"IF YOU'D STOP SNEAKING UP ON ME, JACK, then I wouldn't always be dropping things," Mariah said.

"Get down from there," he ordered. "You don't know what you're doing."

She complied, surprising him with her cooperation as she carefully made her way down the ten-foot ladder. He reached out when she was halfway, unable to stop himself from seizing her by the waist and setting her on the floor in front of him. He didn't release her. Instead, his hold on her tightened. "Stay off that thing!"

"Quit shouting at me. You aren't responsible for me—"

"I'm responsible for everything that happens in this place." His fingers dug into her waist and he jerked her forward so that her hips slammed against him. His response was instant, and he didn't try to conceal it. Something flared in her eyes, something hot and sultry that contrasted sharply with her all-American girl image. He felt her shiver and knew then that she'd be the most responsive of lovers, but for now he couldn't contain his craving for a taste of her, and claimed her mouth. . . .

WHAT ARE *LOVESWEPT* ROMANCES?

They are stories of true romance and touching emotion. We believe those two very important ingredients are constants in our highly sensual and very believable stories in the LOVESWEPT line. Our goal is to give you, the reader, stories of consistently high quality that may sometimes make you laugh, sometimes make you cry, but are always fresh and creative and contain many delightful surprises within their pages.

Most romance fans read an enormous number of books. Those they truly love, they keep. Others may be traded with friends and soon forgotten. We hope that each LOVESWEPT romance will be a treasure—a "keeper." We will always try to publish

LOVE STORIES YOU'LL NEVER FORGET
BY AUTHORS YOU'LL ALWAYS REMEMBER

The Editors

Loveswept® 681

WINTER HEART

LAURA TAYLOR

BANTAM BOOKS
NEW YORK · TORONTO · LONDON · SYDNEY · AUCKLAND

WINTER HEART

A Bantam Book / April 1994

*If you would be interested in receiving protective vinyl covers for your
Loveswept books, please write to this address for information:*

Loveswept
Bantam Books
P.O. Box 985
Hicksville, NY 11802

ISBN 0-553-44348-8

Published simultaneously in the United States and Canada

Bantam Books are published by Bantam Books, a division of Bantam Doubleday Dell Publishing Group, Inc. Its trademark, consisting of the words
"Bantam Books" and the portrayal of a rooster, is Registered in U.S. Patent
and Trademark Office and in other countries. Marca Registrada. Bantam
Books, 1540 Broadway, New York, New York 10036.

PRINTED IN THE UNITED STATES OF AMERICA

OPM   0 9 8 7 6 5 4 3 2 1

To Paul Wagner,
author, Boat School grad, wing-walker
extraordinaire, and the man who taught me
how to laugh again

ONE

Mariah Chandler stood in the shadows of the verandah, idly sliding her fingertips back and forth across the top of the railing that circled the first story of the dilapidated mansion. She'd always loved the serenity of the early-morning hours, the salty feel of the ocean breeze as it caressed her skin, and the almost ethereal quality of the dense patches of fog clinging to the rolling, tree-covered hills that surrounded the run-down structure. On this particular morning, however, she felt more: a sense of anticipation that thrummed through her.

It grew as she awaited the arrival of Jack McMillan, the contractor who would soon begin the restoration of her late grandmother's summer home. It had taken her almost two years to coordinate the restoration.

She'd researched the zoning and building-permit laws of Santa Barbara County, which was known nationwide for its restrictive codes in order to preserve the environment. Mariah respected the philosophy that the land was a precious commodity, but she had personal plans for the mansion that she didn't want thwarted by complex laws or overzealous public officials.

She'd studied the portfolios of several restoration specialists in her search for the right person for the job, and McMillan's portfolio had immediately captured and held her imagination. Her instincts, as much as his obvious talent, assured her that he would understand what she wanted done, and Mariah Chandler was a woman who had learned long ago, and at great personal cost, to trust her instincts.

Securing Jack McMillan's signature on a contract had taken more than a year, however. He was in constant demand and getting on his calendar required patience, but her attorney and the local director of the Chandler Foundation, Bill Witherspoon, had finally negotiated the restoration contract on her behalf.

Closing her eyes for a moment, she calmed herself by breathing deeply of the salty ocean breeze and hibiscus blossoms. She'd slept well during the two nights she'd spent in the estate's refurbished gardener's cottage since her arrival in Santa Barbara, and she looked forward to the three-month respite she'd finally managed to carve out of her demanding schedule.

Mariah loved her position as national director of the Chandler Foundation, but she felt exhausted after four years of never-ending meetings and the nonstop travel necessitated by her work on behalf of victims of spousal abuse. She planned to check in with the D.C. national office on a regular basis during her extended holiday, but she was determined to concentrate on overseeing the restoration. It would be her personal tribute to her late grandmother.

She smiled when she heard a truck round the final curve in the six-mile-long rutted road that wound through the acreage surrounding the mansion. Several moments later a late-model truck pulled into the weed-choked front yard, the logo emblazoned on its side confirming Jack McMillan's identity.

He exited the truck and slammed the door behind him. Tall, broad-shouldered, and lean-hipped, he moved with fluid grace as he crossed the yard. Even in his casual attire of cowboy boots, snug-fitting jeans, and an unzipped leather bomber jacket over a blindingly white T-shirt, Jack McMillan exuded a predatory kind of power that Mariah found jarring and very disconcerting. As he drew nearer, his long-legged stride sent an unspoken message of masculine confidence.

Mariah backed deeper into the shadows of the verandah, seeking time to deal with her awareness of Jack McMillan and to tame her suddenly racing pulse. Until now, she'd thought of him only as a talented restorer. Until now, she'd dismissed the notion that she would ever meet a man who could make her feel capable of passion.

Fascinated by him in spite of an instinctive wariness born of past experiences, Mariah watched the breeze tug at his dark hair. She scanned his tanned, strong-boned face, her gaze skimming over his large hazel eyes, the thick dark brows above them, and his high cheekbones. She viewed the strength of his hard jaw and the sensual shape of his lips, her imagination suggesting that the feel and taste of him would be pure, unadulterated pleasure.

Then suddenly she sensed something familiar about Jack McMillan. Pressing her palms together, Mariah stared at him. Comprehension dawned. Abruptly. Painfully. Shock and disbelief held her immobile as he climbed the steps to the verandah. She blinked, certain she was mistaken, praying she was wrong as memories carried her back into the past.

Mariah drew in a shallow breath. Then another. She felt as though she'd just been slapped across the face. The sting penetrated her soul and wounded her heart.

She kept staring, even as he spoke to her. She heard his deep voice, his Virginia heritage evident in his accent, but she failed to grasp his words. She watched him frown, even understood his confusion as he tried to get a good look at her. She felt the force of his curiosity, and she experienced a moment of gratitude that the shadows prevented him from seeing much more than an outline of her shape.

Mariah knew the next move was hers. Summoning the inner strength that had aided her in her personal life and fueled her commitment to the Chandler Foundation, she reminded herself that she'd come too far to turn back now. Too many people depended on her. Indulging in emotional cowardice wasn't an option worthy of consideration. She couldn't, *wouldn't*, back down from this test of the life and identity she'd built for herself.

"I'm Jack McMillan, Mrs. Chandler," he said, extending his hand. "Are you feeling all right?"

Mariah hesitated. He looked understandably perplexed by her behavior, and she felt a spark of compassion for him. Squaring her shoulders, she stepped forward into a pool of pale sunlight. She accepted his handshake and softly said, "Jackson

McMillan Wainright the Third. It's been a very long time."

He flinched, his fingers closing tightly over hers. In disbelief he peered down at her through narrowed hazel eyes—eyes that reminded her of shards of ice.

Silence reigned. His grip tightened even more, but Mariah didn't try to pull free. She felt the hard calluses on his palms, the heat flowing from his long narrow fingers into her skin, and smelled the seductive scents of soap and a musky men's cologne. Her senses responded instantly. Shaken, Mariah concentrated on not betraying her thoughts and emotions.

Memories continued to flood her mind. Seeing him after so many years forced her to grapple with them, because she sensed that she couldn't just shove them back into some obscure compartment of her mind. Although she'd healed in body and spirit long ago, her memories were a part of the fabric of her life, not simply the catalyst for her dedication to the goals of the foundation she headed.

"It's been at least ten years," Jack finally said.

"Eleven." Lifting her chin, she thought about her wedding day, the first and last time she'd ever been in the company of her former brother-in-law. He'd made an appearance at the reception, and they'd been introduced. They'd spoken to each other very briefly. Mariah recalled her innocence on that day, and how quickly it had been destroyed. She paled. How she hated remembering how trusting she'd been in those days—like a lamb being led to slaughter.

"Meeting this way after so many years is very unexpected," Mariah offered. She studied his unyielding features, searching for a hint of compassion, but she found none in the hard curves and harsh planes of his angular face.

He gave her a scathing look. "Is it?"

"Yes, it is." Mariah attempted to disengage her hand, causing Jack to glance down. Shock flashed in his eyes when he registered their physical connection. He instantly released her.

Hostility emanated from him, and even as she wondered why, she attempted to lessen the tension arcing between them like a live electrical wire. "I knew you'd left Washington, but I didn't realize you were living out here now."

"Didn't you?" Jack demanded, his expression filled with such distaste that Mariah took a step backward.

"No, I did not." A lot of people are depending on me, she reminded herself as she walked to the open front door. "Shall we take a quick tour of the house? We have a lot of work ahead of us, and I'm eager to get under way as soon as possible."

His expression hardened even more. He didn't move, just kept his eyes on her.

Mariah tried once more to break down the invisible barrier between them. "I've toured several examples of your work. I was very impressed when I saw the Bayard mansion in San Francisco and the Alexander estate in San Diego. You're extremely talented."

"You've been busy," he remarked.

Mariah gripped the edge of the door. "I'm thorough, that's all. Did you have a chance to go over the original architecture plans I shipped to you? I researched the house in great detail and found a fairly lengthy list of the materials used by the first builder. Some of the suppliers are still in business after all these years." She smiled as she warmed to the subject of the restoration.

"I'm also very thorough, Ms. Chandler, and I do my own research."

She ignored the razor-sharp edge in his voice and stepped into the entry hall, glancing over her shoulder as she spoke. "Please call me Mariah," she encouraged when he followed her inside.

"Why?"

She turned to face him. "Because Mariah is my name."

"Then why sign everything M. K. Lacey Chandler?"

"I'm usually on the run, and Mariah Kathleen Lacey Chandler takes forever to write."

"Why the subterfuge?"

Baffled, she said, "Subterfuge?"

"Why didn't you want me to know your true identity?"

"That's an odd question, especially since I have nothing whatsoever to hide."

"I want an answer."

Mariah bristled at his dictatorial tone. "I wasn't hiding my identity. I have no need to do anything like that. You, on the other hand, apparently do."

"We aren't talking about me."

"Perhaps we should be."

He turned around and started to walk away. Mariah knew she had to stop him for the sake of the restoration. She forced herself to settle down before she opened her mouth again. "We should be discussing the mansion. It's the only relevant issue between us."

He paused, his broad shoulders filling the wide doorway. Mariah studied his rigid posture and clenched fists for several moments. "Are you always so hostile?" The question slipped past her lips before she could stop it.

He jerked around and glared at her. "I'm not hostile unless I'm being manipulated."

"I don't manipulate, and I don't play games.

I have neither the time nor the energy to waste on that kind of behavior."

Jack glanced at her hand. "You aren't married any longer. Why?"

Although taken aback by his question, she answered him. "I was divorced more than five years ago. My marriage is a closed chapter in my life, and I intend to keep it that way." Mariah marshaled her self-control and continued speaking in a more subdued tone of voice. "We've both just had a surprise, so why don't we simply move beyond it? It's not as though we even had a relationship. Eleven years ago you attended my wedding to your stepbrother. We exchanged less than thirty words that day, and you moved away a short time later. We never saw each other again. No one knew why you left your wife and abandoned your career, but you've obviously started a new life. So have I. End of story."

"You're very defensive," Jack observed a few moments later, his manner still guarded.

"I could make the same observation."

"Don't. You won't score any points, and you need me a hell of a lot more than I need you, Mariah Kathleen Lacey Chandler."

Her temper flared. "I don't walk on eggshells for anyone, Mister McMillan, and that includes you. I gave up that kind of behavior a long time ago, and I don't intend to backpedal now."

"Careful, Ms. Chandler. You're on shaky ground again."

"Mariah," she reminded him once more. "I'm not your sister-in-law or your child, so do not instruct me regarding my attitude or my tone of voice. I am, after all, your employer."

"That remains to be seen." Jack's voice sounded like grinding gears.

She hesitated. She knew that personality conflicts occurred in life and in business, but far more was at stake at the moment. She could take the easy way out and cancel the contract, but she'd worked too hard to make the reconstruction of the mansion a reality, and too many shattered lives needed rebuilding. Chandler House would eventually serve those needs.

Mariah decided to ignore Jack's less than subtle threat to withdraw from the project. She directed her remarks, instead, to her vision of what the interior of the mansion should look like as she walked from room to room on the first floor of the spacious, high-ceilinged dwelling.

Jack followed her, listening to her comments, saying little, and keeping his distance. Mariah's extensive research showed in every word she spoke, as did her knowledge of the restoration process. Once they made their way up to the second story, she turned to him.

"I want the atmosphere to be warm and

welcoming. I intend to avoid the more formal decorating style traditionally used in a Victorian home, in favor of a more relaxed, family-oriented decor typical of country estates."

"Getting married again?"

Startled, she said, "Of course not. Why would you think that?"

Jack shrugged. "Just curious."

"Oh." Still disconcerted, she turned abruptly and began walking down the second-story hallway.

"Mariah!"

She flinched. She hated being yelled at. It reminded her too much of a time in her life when she'd been subjected to constant ridicule. "Don't—"

Before she could turn and tell him not to shout at her, Mariah felt his hands on her. His fingers dug into her narrow waist as he pulled her back against him. She resisted his hold on her, but he easily subdued her as he hauled her back down the hallway.

Jack released her as suddenly as he'd seized her—but not before she'd absorbed the strength and power of his muscled body. Beneath her clothes, her skin tingled from his touch. How, she wondered, could she react so wildly to a man she barely knew?

Although she still felt weak in the knees and

her pulse galloped from his touch, she whirled on him. "Don't ever yell at me again, and don't grab me from behind."

Jack simply looked past her. Shaken and bewildered by his stony gaze, Mariah glanced back over her shoulder. Rotten floorboards gaped open at intervals along the length of the shadowed hallway.

Mariah was embarrassed by her own careless-ness, embarrassed even more by her fear that he might have sensed her reckless response to his touch. She worked at calming herself, all the while eyeing Jack as he peered back at her. She sensed that he rarely, if ever, explained himself to anyone. Mariah wondered yet again why he seemed so angry with her. Before she could ask, Jack turned and made his way back down the staircase.

She followed him, thoroughly baffled by his attitude. As she descended the staircase she recalled her wedding day. Clad in a dark, double-breasted suit, Jackson McMillan Wainright III had seemed the epitome of affluence and self-confidence. A man who seemed to have it all, including an elegant woman on his arm. His wife. A sophisticated, auburn-haired beauty named Delia. Mariah remembered the envy she'd experienced as she'd observed how he'd looked at Delia—with devotion, passion, possession. The kind of covetous looks on a man's face that Mariah had never inspired. She seriously doubted she ever would.

Feeling foolish, she reclaimed what remained of her poise, shifted her attention back to the purpose of their meeting, and crossed the foyer. She barely noticed the water-damaged walls and peeling wallpaper as she joined him in what had once been an elegant sitting room. "I want the mansion restored."

Jack stood in the center of the room, feet apart and arms crossed over his broad chest. He appeared formidable enough to take on an army single-handedly. "I assumed that."

"Then you'll begin on schedule?" she asked.

"I'm not sure I want to begin this project."

"Why not?"

"My reasons don't concern you, Ms. Chandler."

"Of course they do." Mariah stepped into the room. "Look, I'm not going to pretend to understand your attitude. You obviously don't like me. I don't know why, but it isn't really my problem. It's yours. In the meantime, I've done my homework. The building supplies have been ordered and delivered to your warehouse, the blueprints have been filed and the permits are in order, we aren't in danger of violating any reconstruction ordinances, and you have accepted and cashed a substantial check from me that will fund the initial restoration phase of Chandler House. You have a full crew, and the clock is ticking as of next Monday. Now, have I missed something?"

He moved forward, looming over her and studying her with a cynical expression. Mariah held her ground, then ran out of patience when several seconds passed without a response from him. "Aren't you going to say anything?" she asked.

"What do you want me to say?"

"That you're ready to begin. That Chandler House is on your calendar."

He shrugged as though he hadn't a care in the world.

"Jackson—"

"Mr. McMillan," he reminded her.

"Fine. Mr. McMillan, I don't understand—"

"Then don't try."

"I don't remember you as rude."

His jaw tightened. He walked out of the sitting room, the heels of his boots striking the hardwood floor like angry punctuation marks. Mariah refused to give up. She followed him out to the verandah as she considered her options. Abandon the dream she'd nurtured since her grandmother's death, or deal with a hostile man reputed to be the best in the restoration business—a man who, in the space of fifteen minutes, had tantalized her and aroused needs deep in her soul that she'd thought lost to her forever.

She automatically dismissed the former option. Mind made up, Mariah spoke. "Chandler House deserves the very best. You are the best."

"So this is one of your pet projects?"

"Does it matter?" Mariah asked.

"With someone like you, it matters."

She frowned. Someone like me? What does he mean? she wondered. "It shouldn't matter. Nothing should matter other than the mansion."

"I'm having second thoughts."

"But you've already agreed to do the job. Your second thoughts might be awkward for us both," she remarked, her reminder that they had a signed contract he couldn't just ignore less than subtle.

"Why me?" he demanded.

Mariah gave him a look designed to reduce a large boulder to dust. "I want the best," she said very slowly, steel etched into each and every word. "I can afford the best. *You* are the best."

He scowled at her. "Why are you restoring the mansion? It's been neglected for years."

Mariah felt reluctant to reveal her personal motives. "Don't you think it would be a shame not to restore it?"

He ignored her question. "Bill Witherspoon said you inherited the property."

Mariah nodded, cautious but still willing to admit a partial truth. "That's right. From my grandmother."

His gaze narrowed speculatively. "You're bored, aren't you? You have money to burn, and you're at loose ends."

Mariah almost laughed out loud. She couldn't recall a time in her life when she'd ever been bored. Inactivity didn't suit her. It never had. "You couldn't be more wrong, but I'm not the issue. The mansion is, and I'm committed to the restoration."

"I'm not," he said bluntly.

"What exactly does that mean?"

"Precisely what I just said." He walked away from her then, and he didn't look back as he descended the verandah steps and made his way to his truck.

Mariah followed him, unwilling to be put off by his rudeness or his threats. "I'll expect you on Monday morning," she called out.

He glanced at her after climbing into his truck. "I'll be in touch in a few days. I'll let you know then whether or not I'm willing to do the job." He revved the powerful engine, shoved it into gear, and drove off, leaving her standing in a cloud of dust.

She blurted out an unladylike word before shouting, "We have a contract, Jackson McMillan Wainright the Third, and you're going to honor it even if I have to drag you into court!"

TWO

At the end of the third day following her confrontation with Jack McMillan, Mariah left the West Coast office of the Chandler Foundation and stepped into the elevator of one of the few high-rise buildings in Santa Barbara. After the double doors slid closed, she lowered her heavy briefcase to the floor and leaned back against the wall.

She sighed, the soft sound the only evidence of her fatigue following a marathon meeting. Glad that her workday was finally over, Mariah undid her French braid. Her honey-colored hair tumbled free, cascading over her shoulders and down to the center of her back, her bangs fluffing as she finger-combed the strands away from her face.

The elevator paused just seconds later. The doors opened, and a man stepped into the elevator. Mariah froze, her hands falling to her sides.

Jack McMillan frowned but said nothing. He was brooding over the advice his lawyer had just given him—that he honor the contract he'd signed with Mariah's representatives. And now Mariah was here, and he couldn't help but resent her.

He'd learned the hard way that women like her never did anything without a selfish motive. Beautiful creatures without a thought for anybody except themselves. They pretended to care about others, but only if it brought them attention. He'd been a fool before and suffered greatly at the hands of one, but he'd be damned if he'd let himself be duped again.

Jack stabbed the down button, then turned his gaze to Mariah. When the tip of her tongue darted out to moisten her lower lip, he wondered if the gesture was innocent, if she knew how provocative it was. She was the most innately sensual woman he'd met in years, even though she dressed conservatively, had spoken to him like a drill sergeant during their encounter at the Chandler estate, and possessed an attitude of superiority that made him want to grab her and shake her until she let down her guard enough to admit her true motive for hiring him to restore the Chandler mansion.

Heat and desire suddenly gushed into his bloodstream like a flash flood. Startled by his body's response to her, Jack swore soundlessly and pushed a second button on the elevator's control panel. The small cubicle shuddered to an abrupt stop.

Mariah's eyes widened. She stiffened under Jack's intent gaze. He thought she looked rigid enough to snap under the pressure of a gentle breeze.

"What are you doing?" Her eyes darted between the control panel and his face.

"Stopping the damn elevator."

"Why? There are people in this building who need to use it." As if to emphasize her remark, she glanced up at the red lights blinking above the closed doors.

"They can wait."

"Were you looking for me?" she asked.

"Hardly."

Mariah took a shallow breath, then another. Jack observed the rapid rise and fall of her full breasts beneath the white silk tunic she wore over matching slacks.

"Are you claustrophobic?"

She looked bewildered, but she answered him anyway. "Of course not."

"Then breathe normally before you pass out. Considering the day I've just had, the last thing I want or need is to have to deal with some female who can't stand on her own two feet."

Mariah flushed. Opening her clenched fists, she pressed her palms back against the wall of the elevator. She lifted her chin. "This is a surprise, our meeting this way."

He ignored her comment. "Your color's coming back."

"Thank you for telling me," she said with sarcasm.

"What is it with you?"

"I don't know what you mean."

"Don't you?"

She shook her head. Her hair shifted over her shoulders. An errant tendril caressed her cheek. Jack felt the heat in his blood rise several degrees. The urge to touch the silky strand made his fingers itch. Damn her, he thought.

"Lady, you set my teeth on edge."

"Why?" she whispered.

She looked so guileless, but then so had Delia, and Delia had had the morals and instincts of an alley cat. "I'll be damned if I know."

"Maybe—"

"There's no maybe about it."

Jack took a step in her direction. "Don't stiffen up on me that way, and keep breathing. You aren't afraid of me. I can see that much in your eyes."

Mariah's chin rose another notch. Jack saw belligerence and something more filter into her gaze, but he couldn't quite discern the something more. He intended to, though.

"Why would I be afraid of you?" she asked. "From what I've seen, you're just one more man with a surly nature and a short temper. The fact that your talent manages to surface every now and then is nothing short of amazing."

He smiled. "The cat has claws. If you're not afraid, then what are you?"

"Are you trying to confuse me, or do you speak to everyone this way?"

"I'm trying to figure you out."

"Perhaps you shouldn't try. Haven't you ever heard the old cliché—what you see is what you get."

He moved closer, and what he saw in her widening gaze made his senses go on alert.

"Now what are you doing?" she asked.

He shrugged, glad he possessed the power to make her uneasy. She'd thrown his world into instant turmoil three days ago. It was her turn, he decided. Her turn to feel off-balanced by things she couldn't control with her checkbook or her family connections. He refused to have anyone from the past destroy all that he'd worked for and achieved. Whatever her motive, he intended to know the truth. And if she was in league with his stepbrother, then God help her, because he'd stop her in her tracks before she knew what hit her. The fact that she was divorced from Darren meant nothing and proved even less.

He finally answered her question. "I'm not altogether sure what I'm going to do, but I'll let you know when I figure it out."

"This is ridiculous." Mariah glanced at her watch. "I . . . I have an appointment, and you're about to make me late for it."

Jack stepped in front of her as she straightened and eyed the elevator's control panel. Mariah paused.

"You're lying, but even if you aren't, the appointment can wait."

"You have more nerve—" she began.

"You're right, and I'm glad you approve." He placed his large hands atop her shoulders.

"I don't approve, and you know it."

She felt fragile beneath his fingers and palms. "You're small."

"I'm not small. I'm five feet, six inches tall. Quite average," she insisted in a tight little whisper. "What exactly are you trying to prove? That you're bigger and stronger than I am? Well, I concede the obvious."

"I'm not trying to prove anything, but I'll let you know if I change my mind."

She blinked, but didn't move. She exhaled a

moment later, the sound faintly tattered, achingly seductive. He lowered his head, his gaze riveted on her face. He studied her intently, waiting, watching, reading the emotions in her eyes. When her indignation disappeared, he recognized an expression akin to hunger. He felt hungry too. Hell, he felt ravenous, and it suddenly mattered more than it should have that she was responding to him. He couldn't ignore her, even though he knew he was crazy to even touch her.

A moan escaped her. An erotic moan, part invitation, part disbelief, but not a protest, he realized triumphantly. Her gaze swept across his face, then settled on his lips. He edged closer, the air trapped in his chest starting to burn. When her hands flattened against his abdomen, he paused, waiting for her to push, expecting the rejection that had to happen next. She might not realize it, but his conscience wouldn't allow him to ignore her wishes.

She didn't push against him, though. Instead, she kneaded the hard muscles beneath her fingertips.

"I'm going to kiss you," he said in a whisper.

"I know," she whispered back. "I just don't understand why."

That makes two of us.

She dug her fingers into the front of his shirt.

He wondered if she knew what she was doing to him. Rivers of fire raced through his veins, and his body hardened even more. He ached inside, and he realized that no one had made him feel this way in years.

"You don't even like me," she continued. "And you seem to think I've got some kind of hidden agenda, which, for the record, I don't."

"You're right. I don't like you, and I don't trust you."

"Why would you—"

He kissed her then, intending to chastise, determined to let her know that he wouldn't be used, but he failed miserably. It stunned him, this need to be gentle, this need to possess with tenderness. He felt her go absolutely still beneath his hands and lips. Shock, he decided, and not distaste. He explored, he tantalized, and he aroused, all without going beyond the seam of her trembling lips. And he wondered with every second that ticked by why he craved the taste of her.

When he finally released her lips, every pulse point in his body throbbed, the heat coursing through him threatened to become an inferno, and the ache in his loins made him shudder. He lifted his head, his eyes falling closed as he ground his teeth.

He didn't want to want her. He hated the

weakness within himself that drew him to beautiful shallow women who used and manipulated, and then betrayed. No matter how beautifully wrapped the package, the contents invariably inflicted pain. He'd learned that lesson only after enduring immeasurable pain.

Mariah suddenly trembled beneath his hands. He opened his eyes and looked at her. Either she was one hell of an actress, or the kiss had affected her as much as it had him.

"Will you do the job you've agreed to do?" she asked, the sound of her voice like a caress, the actual words a bomb blast on an otherwise silent day.

He released her and raked his fingers through his hair. "You're good."

"Will you?" she asked, her voice low and intense.

Her nerve and determination astounded him. Unwilling to lose control of his temper, Jack stabbed the release button. He stood with his arms crossed over his chest as the elevator resumed its descent.

"Jack . . . you're not being reasonable about—"

"Lunch," he cut in. "Tomorrow at noon. The place is called The Tavern. Be there if you want my answer."

"Wouldn't it be easier on both of us if you gave me your answer now?"

"Be there."

She hesitated, her reluctance apparent, then nodded. "All right."

He didn't look back as he exited the elevator at the next stop and took the stairs the rest of the way to the parking garage. Convinced that she viewed his invitation as a personal triumph, he savored the idea of having Mariah Chandler on his turf. Bringing her down a notch or two, he decided, was exactly what she needed.

She hated the place on sight, but she made herself get out of her car and walk into The Tavern. It was a dive. Although Mariah had never been in one before, she recognized it for what it was.

"Hey, baby! Slumming today? Come on over here and let old Leroy give you a thrill."

An array of similar remarks and loud guffaws followed Leroy's crude offer. Mariah flinched, but she kept walking, her spine rigid as she threaded her way through the crowded bar in search of an empty table.

She grasped Jack's motive for selecting such a disreputable place for their lunch meeting. His challenge was obvious, and she intended to respond to it. Nothing and no one—not even the rowdy, leering patrons of The Tavern—

would prevent her from forcing him to honor the contract he'd signed.

The lewd comments, bursts of ribald laughter, and strutting forays past her table continued. But aside from being given a menu and a sympathetic look from a harried-looking waitress, she was approached by no one.

Mariah kept her expression even and her eyes glued to the menu gripped in her hands. She simmered in silence for five of the longest minutes of her life. An old hand at being the target of deliberate embarrassment and humiliation, Mariah planned her next move.

Jack spotted the white Mercedes as he pulled into the rutted parking lot of The Tavern. He smiled, satisfied that she'd arrived ahead of him. Calmer than he'd been the previous day, he almost regretted selecting the tacky establishment as the location for lunch with a woman like Mariah Chandler. Almost, but not quite.

The instant he spotted her, alone at a table in the center of the dimly lighted, noisy, barnlike building, his footsteps slowed. His satisfaction faded when he noticed her white-knuckled grip on the menu and her strained but composed expression. Mariah was as out of place at The Tavern as he knew she'd be, but that realization gave him little of the pleasure he had anticipated. Jack suddenly felt like a first-class jerk, and he didn't like the feeling at all.

He listened for a moment to the catcalls and whistles directed her way. As he watched her chin rise he gave her high marks for holding on to her dignity by the sheer force of her will. He also felt admiration for her courage and inner strength, but his suspicions about her motives refused to ease.

Jack made his way through the crowd, nodding as several people greeted him or slapped him on the back. He kept his attention focused on Mariah, who didn't bother to look at him as he pulled out a chair and sat down opposite her.

"Have you ordered yet?"

Mariah lifted her gaze from the menu and shook her head. The catcalls continued. Jack glowered at several of the men lined up at the bar. Their voices lowered instantly, their attention shifting away from Mariah.

She didn't acknowledge the altered mood or behavior of the patrons in the restaurant. Shifting in his chair, Jack welcomed the waitress with an easy smile. He ordered the house special, a burger with everything on it, and then glanced expectantly at Mariah.

Tight-lipped, Mariah dug into her purse, extracted a crisp twenty-dollar bill, and slapped it on the table as she got to her feet. "Enjoy your meal. Leave the change for"—she glanced at the woman's name tag—"Millie. She deserves it." She walked away without another word.

The waitress grinned and snatched up the twenty from the tabletop. "You blew it, Jack. She's a lady."

Jack watched Mariah make her way through the crowded watering hole, amazed as the construction workers and truckers who frequented the place created a path for her. She was elegance personified in tailored leather slacks and a beaded silk blouse; her carriage and the measured pace of her footsteps gave her a regal air.

Feeling like a fool, Jack pushed himself to his feet just as she reached the front door, jerked it open, and disappeared from sight. Seconds later he stepped out into the bright California sunshine and followed her at a half jog. His conscience suggested an apology was in order for the stunt he'd just pulled.

"Hey, Vassar, hold on a minute. We need to talk."

She paused at her car, but she didn't bother to look at him as she ransacked her purse. "Talk to your friends. I don't have time to waste on your games."

He came up behind her, settling one hand on her shoulder just as she found her keys.

Mariah shrugged free of him and unlocked the car door. Jack forced her to hold still, his hands like heavy anchors on her shoulders, then turned her around.

"Take your hands off me." She was seething, her blue eyes shooting sparks of pure fury at him.

His apology turned to ashes in his mouth. He removed his hands, but he didn't step away from her.

"I will not be intimidated by you. Do you understand me?"

"Loud and clear. I was out of line," he admitted.

Mariah dismissively waved her hand in his direction. Jack fell silent, aware that he deserved her anger.

"I've been put down, manipulated, and demeaned by experts. You need to polish your skills if you're going to make a habit of this kind of behavior."

Her comments stung, but he couldn't deny the truth. He'd wanted to put her down, and he'd wanted her to feel manipulated. Jack nodded. "You're right."

"Why? What was the point of this little exercise? I keep telling you that I don't have a hidden agenda, but you refuse to take me at my word. Why not stop all this nonsense and get on with the restoration? It's all I want from you, and it's all I'll ever want from a man like you."

A man like me? What the hell did she mean by a statement like that? he wondered. "I find that very hard to believe."

"I've done nothing inappropriate, and I have no interest in you or the choices you've made in your life. I've simply hired you to do a job. The fact that we were introduced several years ago has nothing whatsoever to do with our current association. This is business, pure and simple. Why do you insist on making this situation into something it's not?"

"We need to talk about the contract."

"I'm finished talking," she announced.

"I don't trust you," he said once again.

She looked up at him, shock in her eyes. The kind of shock, he realized, that couldn't be faked. A part of him actually wanted to believe her when she insisted that she didn't have a secret agenda, but the past made him very wary.

Mariah asked, "You're serious, aren't you?"

"I couldn't be more serious."

"This isn't about trust. This is about honoring commitments. You've made a commitment to me, and I expect you to honor it."

Mariah jerked open her car door. Jack slammed the door shut. She glared at him. He glared right back at her.

"I said we need to talk."

"There's nothing left to talk about. Today is Saturday. You're scheduled to begin the restoration in forty-eight hours, and I expect it to happen on time. If it doesn't, you will be in violation of the contract you signed. I will then sue you."

"Don't threaten me," he gritted out.

"Then don't force my hand."

"I do not like your type, Mariah Chandler."

"I'm not a type. I'm a person. Besides, you don't even know me, so don't presume to judge me and don't attempt to categorize me as some airhead who hasn't got the sense to come in out of the rain. It's women like me who actually get things accomplished in this world. Join the twentieth century before it ends, why don't you? Otherwise, you'll miss the progress we're making."

"You're not making any sense," he accused.

"Aren't I? I think I'm making perfect sense." She pulled open the car door a second time and slipped into the driver's seat before he could stop her. "I'll see you at the mansion. If I don't, then you can deal with my attorney."

He watched her drive out of the parking lot, his gaze locked on her vehicle until it disappeared from sight around a sharp curve in the road.

He spent the remainder of the day and the

weekend in turmoil over the fact that he had no choice but to begin restoring the Chandler mansion on Monday morning. But even as he rued the moment he'd signed the contract, he couldn't dismiss the desire Mariah Chandler provoked within him. It ate at him ceaselessly, robbing him of sleep at night and prompting anyone who crossed his path during the next several days to give him a very wide berth.

THREE

Relieved when the restoration began on schedule, Mariah confined her visits to the mansion to the early-morning hours before Jack and his crew arrived for work that first week. She didn't wish to aggravate him or provoke another confrontation, but she still intended to accomplish the tasks she'd established for herself.

Mariah stuck to her original plan of photographically documenting each step of the reconstruction process, in response to requests from both national and state historical societies and because of her own personal passion for the project. She also began making as many of the decorating decisions as she could before engaging the services of a professional decorator.

Armed with her camera, paint chips, wallpaper samples, and a thermos of hot chocolate, she arrived each morning well before dawn. She made use of her time by photographing and diagraming each room so that she could plan the furnishings. By keeping a close eye on her watch, she left the mansion just minutes before Jack and his workmen arrived each day.

The two upper floors of the mansion contained a total of ten bedrooms, as many bathrooms, and suitable space for a playroom at the end of each upstairs hallway. Although the floors and walls were a mess, she had little trouble imagining what the rooms would eventually look like. Hospitable, attractive, upbeat, they would be a very welcome change for the women and children who would be their occupants.

On this early Sunday morning Mariah carefully skirted several ruptured sections of flooring as she made her way to an open window in an upstairs bedroom. With the aid of the sunshine that flooded the room, she studied a selection of floral wallpaper samples, making periodic notes to herself on a small pad of paper.

She took her time, assuming that she had the entire day to herself. When she heard the soft purr of a car engine a few minutes later, she glanced out the window. A sleek imported vehicle the color of a shiny red apple pulled into the front yard. Mariah recognized the driver the instant he got out of the car.

She instinctively stepped backward when Jack McMillan looked up, his gaze roaming across the front of the mansion. She lost her footing as the heel of her shoe sank into a gap between two rotten planks of wood. The wallpaper samples flew from her hands as she lost her balance and fell.

She landed hard. Wood crackled and snapped beneath her, and her foot wound up wedged between the two planks. She gingerly tried to free her trapped foot, but the sound of footsteps coming up the staircase stilled her movements.

Jack appeared in the doorway to the room. "I thought I warned you about wandering around up here. It's a construction site, not the local museum."

Mariah nodded, mollified by the gentle tone of voice. "You did warn me, and your concern was justified. Now that I've admitted you were right, would you mind helping me out of this hole? My foot's stuck, and I'm afraid I'm going to make the situation worse if I try to do this on my own."

Tears flooded her eyes, startling her. She blinked them away, determined not to embarrass herself any further.

Jack inspected the floor with experienced eyes as he slowly circled around behind her. She felt relieved that he made no further comment about the fact that she'd ignored his directive to stay out of the mansion. She sighed softly and shoved at the wisps of pale hair that had come loose from her ponytail.

"Raise your hands above your head," he told her. "When I have a good grip on your wrists, I want you to turn your right foot about three inches to the left and then point your toes. Once your foot is free, I'm going to lift you straight up and out. Don't worry if some of the flooring gives way as you work your foot loose. Understand?"

She nodded and lifted her arms. She immediately felt his strength as he took hold of her wrists and held her suspended above the gaping hole in the floor. When he lowered her a few inches, she shifted her foot and successfully freed it.

Jack lifted her easily, bringing her up and away from the damaged timbers and into his arms. He held her so tightly for a moment, she nearly stopped breathing. Her heart thudded wildly; its frantic beat matched by the pounding of his own.

Looping her arms around his neck, he picked her up and carried her out of the bedroom and down the long hallway. Once they reached the staircase, she said, "There's no need for you to carry me. I can walk on my own now."

"Humor me," Jack suggested.

The sound of his voice took a toll on her. It was so gritty, so incredibly low and sexy, she almost groaned. Feeling shaky, she took a deep breath to calm herself—and inhaled the seductive fragrance of his clean, musk-scented skin. She realized that she didn't want him to let her go before it was absolutely necessary.

Mariah studied Jack's angular profile from beneath partially lowered eyelashes, her memory flashing back to those stunning moments in the elevator when he'd kissed her. His tenderness had devastated her, just as the security she found in his embrace devastated her now. She wondered if he knew what sweet torture it was for her to be in his arms as he made his way down the stairs, across the foyer, and into the gutted kitchen on the first floor of the mansion.

Jack settled her atop a stool that had been left in the kitchen. Stepping back, he dropped to one knee and began unlacing the athletic shoe on her right foot.

"I'm all right," she protested. "Really."

He didn't even look at her as he removed her shoe, peeled off her sock, and cupped her foot so that her heel rested in the palm of his large, callused hand.

"Wiggle your toes."

She did, a faint smile edging up the sides of her mouth.

"Arch your foot."

She did that, too, her gaze skimming across the width of his shoulders and then settling on his thick dark hair. "I'm fine. Nothing's broken."

He glanced at her, his expression unrevealing. "We'll see."

"Yes, Doctor." Her smile broadened when he suddenly scowled at her.

He kept his dark-eyed gaze on her. She stared back at him, tingling sensation rioting in her bloodstream as he slid his fingertips across and then under her arch. Her smile faded as his gentle fingers left a trail of glittering heat in their wake.

Mariah shuddered, then sank her teeth into her lower lip to keep herself from moaning at the pleasure she experienced from his touch. She also closed her hands into fists, thwarting the impulse she felt to place her hands on his shoulders. She didn't want him to know that no man had ever treated her with such care or tenderness. Neither did she want him to realize that he aroused her with his innocent handling of her foot and ankle.

When Jack closed his fingers around her ankle, she winced, the pain like a bolt of lightning.

Jack frowned. "That really hurts, doesn't it?"

"It's a little sore," she admitted.

He carefully eased her sock back over her foot, then slipped on her shoe. After tying the laces, he suggested, "Try putting your weight on it." Jack got to his feet and extended his hand.

Mariah accepted his assistance, even though she didn't really need it. She placed her weight on her right foot, gingerly at first, then with more confidence. "I'm fine, just a little embarrassed that I wasn't paying attention to where I was going."

"You were right. You haven't broken anything, but you'll probably have an ugly bruise in a day or two. An ice pack will keep the swelling to a minimum. I can take you to the emergency room if you'd prefer a more qualified diagnosis."

"You seem to know what you're doing, so I don't think a second opinion is necessary."

"It's up to you." He released her and stepped back.

Mariah immediately missed the physical connection. Pressing her palms together in front of her, she said, "Thank you."

"For what?" He jammed his hands into the back pockets of his dark trousers and peered at her curiously.

Her gaze dipped, drawn to the power of his muscular thighs, lean hips, and flat belly. She felt her heart flutter and her pulse pick up speed. His appeal was undeniable, and for a moment she wished he had the physique of a whale and the sensuality of a rock.

"For what, Mariah?" he asked a second time in a lazy, knowing tone of voice.

She met his gaze, unwilling to feel embarrassed that he'd recognized her curiosity for what it was. "Thank you for coming upstairs," she answered. "I would've had a heck of a time getting out of that hole on my own."

"I told you to be careful up there."

"I know, but I have a lot of work to do."

"Do it when I'm here."

"I don't want to get in the way. You're all very busy."

"I meant it when I told you I don't like anyone wandering around the job site. It's dangerous."

"You're repeating yourself . . . again."

"Because you don't listen." He gave her a hard, probing look. "You're stubborn as all hell, aren't you?"

Her chin rose. "Yes, I am. That's how a goal becomes a reality. Look, I have work to do. I can't ignore it any more than you can ignore what you need to do."

"Save it until the restoration's finished."

She shook her head. "I can't. I have to order the paint and wallpaper within the next few weeks. Some of the wallpaper patterns I want to use aren't even available any longer, but I've found a man who's willing to work with sketches."

"Your timing is lousy, Mariah. This is a dangerous location until the floors and walls are stabilized."

"There were color sketches of some of the upstairs bedrooms in my grandmother's personal papers. I know what some of these rooms should look like. I've waited for two years to start this project. I *won't* wait any longer."

Jack walked to the kitchen door under Mariah's watchful gaze. He exhaled, the sound unexpectedly ragged and oddly vulnerable. He stood with his back to her and stared at the remains of what had once been an extensive rose garden behind the mansion.

"Don't try to resurrect the past. It can't be done. Facsimiles are all you can hope to achieve, and they're often nothing more than pale imitations."

"That's an odd thing for you to say."

"I don't re-create the past. I know better than to try. You're old enough and clever enough to have learned that particular lesson by now."

Certain that he was referring to something personal, rather than the restoration of the mansion, she responded as best she could. "I'm not trying to re-create the past."

"Aren't you?" he asked as he slowly turned to face her.

"Absolutely not. The past is over. It should stay that way." The bleakness in his eyes made her want to comfort him.

He studied her for a long while. "Why?"

She got the distinct impression that her answer would be important to him, although she didn't understand why. Mariah drew in a steadying breath as she reflected for a moment on her own complicated personal history. "Reliving it is a mistake. Even when you want to change the past, especially the painful parts, you're stuck with the reality that you can't. I've learned to be content with the here and now, and to look forward to the promise of the future."

She searched his face, but she failed to discern his state of mind or understand his motive for cautioning her about the past. She longed to understand, though, because she sensed that he was revealing something very important about himself, despite the oblique nature of his comments.

"You've been in here every morning since we started, haven't you?"

She hesitated briefly, then admitted the truth. "Yes, I have."

"It would be safer for you and easier on me if you'd show up during working hours. That way someone can keep an eye on you."

"I don't need a baby-sitter."

He glanced at her ankle. "Don't you?"

"No, I do not. What happened upstairs was due to my clumsiness. I'll simply be more careful in the future."

"I'll see that you are."

Mariah put the brakes on her temper and changed the subject. "Would you like some hot chocolate? I still have some left in my thermos."

He gave her a look she didn't understand. When he didn't answer, Mariah made her way to the thermos she'd left atop a stack of lumber on the opposite side of the spacious kitchen. After pouring the hot chocolate into the plastic cup, she approached Jack. She paused in the center of the kitchen, her message clear—she expected him to meet her halfway. He did with obvious reluctance, his footsteps measured, his gaze fixed on her as he moved toward her.

"Is this a peace offering?"

Mariah smiled. She heard something intimate in his low voice, and she couldn't help wondering what it would be like to wake up each morning in the arms of a man like Jack McMillan. The thought, unexpected and more than a little unnerving, sent heat rushing into her veins. Her hand shook as she extended the cup.

"Is it, Mariah?" he pressed.

"I guess it is."

His hand closed around hers, the warmth of his skin adding to the warmth of the plastic cup nestled in her palm. "I don't know what to make of you."

She suddenly felt the urge to lighten the moment, so she quipped, "What you see is . . ."

He moved closer, his hand tightening around hers. " . . . isn't what you are," he finished for her. "Clichés won't cut it with you. You're a lot more . . . complex."

She met his gaze. "You insist on endowing me with motives that don't exist. I'm not what you think I am, whatever that might be."

"You have a thousand and one secrets. They're in your eyes."

She shook her head, denial automatic and instinctive. "Life is complicated enough without us making it even more so. As much as you seem to need to believe that I have ulterior motives for hiring you and for wanting Chandler House restored, I'm not some sinister creature with a hidden agenda."

"You've said that too many times already. Your words sound hollow at this point."

"You're difficult to understand, Jack."

"I'm a simple man."

"You're the most complicated man I've ever encountered." She paused, then voiced the next thought that popped into her head, even though she knew the risk she took. "The woman who hurt you did a real job on you, didn't she?"

He stiffened. She glimpsed his anger as it flashed in his dark eyes. When it faded, she said quietly, "I've been betrayed, too, and I'll even admit to being cautious in most of my relationships, but I try not to hold grudges and I'm not suspicious of every person who crosses my path. I also don't hold total strangers responsible for the actions of other people. Can't you bend a little and give me the benefit of the doubt?"

Jack glanced down at the cup of chocolate. "Is this for me or not?"

She sighed, frustrated by his intransigence. "Of course."

He plucked the cup from her hand, lifted it to his mouth, his gaze intent as he watched her and deliberately drank from the spot with an imprint of her lipstick. Mesmerized by his overtly sensual behavior, suddenly feeling drunk on some erotic stimulant, Mariah stared at him as he drained the cup.

Jack handed her the empty cup, then said, "Stay out of here unless I'm around. Another fall like the one you took a little while ago, and this place could wind up becoming your coffin, not the home you seem to want."

Her heart stuttered to a stop. However insightful his comment, she didn't want him to know that he was right. She craved a real home, because she'd never had one of her own. Shuttled around like a piece of luggage as a child until her late grandmother had stepped in to rescue her from grasping relatives eager to control her inheritance, Mariah had tried and failed to create a home with her former husband. It had taken therapy to understand that the failure had been his.

"I'll be careful. I promise."

"Like today?"

"How about a compromise? I'll come over during working hours, and I'll always check in with you or your foreman. I realize you'll worry about me if I don't."

"José doesn't have time to trail around after you. Neither do I."

"I won't bother him. I won't bother anyone."

"You'd bother a dead man, and you know it." He advanced on her.

She held her ground, although he towered over when he finally stopped. Oddly, she didn't feel threatened.

"You're hot, Mariah Chandler. So hot you sizzle most of the time. You know it, and I know it, and so does any man who looks at you."

Sultry sensations roared in her veins. Once intimidated by raw sexuality in a man, she realized she was responding to Jack McMillan on a primal level. She nearly groaned at the erotic images her mind suddenly produced. Warmth swept up her cheeks, and she had to work hard to keep her breathing steady.

Pretending to be unaffected, she said, "Was that comment necessary?"

"It felt like it was."

"And you do everything you feel like doing?"

He shrugged.

"I think you like being unreasonable, and I think that's sad."

"Don't waste your pity. I don't want it or need it."

Compassion sprang to life inside her. She didn't understand how or why. It was just there, like a piercing shaft of bright light through her heart.

Mariah recalled how defensive she'd once been. She also remembered the patience shown to her by the few people she'd allowed into her life during the early years following the end of her marriage. She knew with utter certainty now that Jack McMillan had been deeply wounded by someone he'd once trusted. She knew that fact almost as well as she knew her own name. She sensed that the someone was a woman. Perhaps Delia, the wife he'd once looked at with possessiveness and adoration.

She smiled. "You're stuck with me, you know. I have no intention of fading into the woodwork just because you don't like me or approve of me."

He frowned, clearly baffled by her shift in attitude. His gaze skimmed over her features as her smile widened. "You're staring. Didn't anyone ever tell you it's rude?"

Mariah turned away from him. She gathered up her thermos and the tote bag filled with paint chips and wallpaper samples. "Now, if you'll excuse me, I'm going to the cottage and do some work."

"Work?" he scoffed. "Rich socialites don't work. They live off the fat of the land and their inheritances."

"Maybe the ones you've known, but don't make the mistake of classifying me as useless, Jack McMillan, because I'm not. I never have been, and I never will be. The only thing I've ever been is innocent and optimistic. I lost my innocence a long time ago. It was beaten out of me in a situation I couldn't control, but I never lost my optimism." Mariah felt her insides tighten with tension, and she consciously calmed herself. "It's a part of me that I'll never relinquish, not for anybody." Satisfied that she'd made her position very clear, she started down the hallway.

"Mariah!" he shouted.

She turned and looked at him. "Yes?"

He studied her for a long moment, as though pondering her, before he gruffly ordered, "Watch yourself around here. I don't need a damn lawsuit on top of everything else."

"I won't sue you unless you fail to fulfill our contract."

"I'm serious. The liability is mine if anything happens to you."

"I won't cause any problems."

"You already have."

"Sorry," she said flippantly. She waved and walked out the front door, calling out over her shoulder, "Enjoy your day."

Mariah strolled back to the gardener's cottage at a leisurely pace. She took pride in the fact that she'd met Jack McMillan head-on and emerged from their verbal fray intact. While her common sense told her to maintain her guard and not become overconfident in her dealings with him, her heart ached with the need to dismantle the barriers he'd constructed against her.

She wrestled with his hostile attitude and the reasons for it for most of the rest of the day. His consistent defensiveness led her to the conclusion that she reminded him of a part of his life he apparently wanted to forget. It was the only logical reason for his behavior. She already knew he'd walked out on his old life more than ten years ago, but she'd never known why. Darren had refused to talk about it when questioned, and she hadn't ever become acquainted with Delia Fleming Wainright following their initial meeting.

Mariah sensed that the only way to deal with Jack was to be as patient as she could be while demonstrating that she posed no threat to his new life or his peace of mind. How she would achieve her goal, she didn't know, but she decided to try. His bark, she'd already discovered, was far worse than his bite. Unlike many of the men she'd encountered in her work in recent years, Jack McMillan was worth the effort, not simply because of his expertise as a restorer, but because she genuinely cared about his emotional well-being.

When her common sense reminded her that she was attracted to him for reasons that had nothing to do with his emotional health, Mariah realized that she would have to keep a tight rein on her own feelings, which seemed to escalate with each meeting.

FOUR

"Hey, boss, there's someone here to see you."

Jack didn't bother to look up from the architectural plans spread out across the drafting table at the end of the first-floor hallway. "I'm busy, Tommy. Tell whoever it is to wait."

The youthful apprentice carpenter, whose penchant for well-endowed women, fast cars, and Mexican beer was legend among his friends, leaned down and lowered his voice. "I sure wouldn't make her wait. She looks good enough to—"

Jack's head snapped up. He didn't need to be told who *she* was. "Where?"

"At the front door. She said she didn't want to disturb you until you took your break, but I told her you wouldn't mind." Tommy smiled, exposing nearly all of his perfect teeth. "I sure wouldn't mind. I get disturbed just looking at her."

Jack scowled, then peered down the hallway. He felt even more raw-nerved when he saw Mariah's smile of greeting. "Don't you have something to do?" he muttered without looking at the young man. "Or do I pay you to stand around and grin at me all day?"

Tommy laughed, then clutched his chest. "Boss! You wound me. You truly do."

"Tell her I'll be with her in a minute, and don't take all day doing it. And tell her to stay put," Jack added, his voice sharp with frustration.

"Yes, sir." Popping a breath mint into his mouth, Tommy swaggered down the hallway.

Jack shook his head and deliberately turned his back on Mariah. As he rolled the sheaf of plans he'd been studying into a tight cylinder, he thought about the wretched night he'd just endured. His body tightened up as erotic images of Mariah started playing through his mind again.

Feeling as frustrated as an adolescent boy, Jack held Mariah Chandler responsible for the sexual tension that constantly invaded his body and robbed him of his peace of mind. Although he realized that he needed a woman, not just any woman would do. Jack knew better than to slake his desire on someone he didn't care about.

He'd given up that kind of careless behavior long ago.

He was damned if he did, and damned if he didn't, he realized.

With his free hand, Jack shoved his fingers through his dark hair. It didn't seem to matter that she set his teeth on edge, because every single time he thought about her, all he really wanted was the feel of her in his arms, naked and clinging to him. He wanted to make her moan with pleasure as he slowly explored the curves and hollows of her shapely body. He wanted to arouse her to a fever pitch and then satisfy her until she lost touch with reality. And then he wanted to do it again. And again, until they were both mindless and replete.

His body reacted to his thoughts, the discomfort he felt making him swear as he shoved the plans into a plastic tube and dropped it into an already crowded bin beside the drafting table. Straightening, he noticed that two of his crew had paused to study him. His stormy facial expression sent them back to work in short order.

Jack had no doubt about his ability to orchestrate the restoration of the fifteen-thousand-square-foot mansion. He'd done larger and far more complicated structures. What he seriously doubted was his ability to deal with Mariah Chandler every step of the way.

She tempted him. Ceaselessly. She inspired a hunger in him for things he hadn't even thought about in recent years. She made him feel emotions he normally sidestepped with ease. She even made him consider abandoning the vow he'd made to himself following Delia's betrayal. And she made him forget at unexpected moments that she'd once been married to his stepbrother, a man who'd robbed him of everything he'd held dear.

Jack summoned his self-control before he turned away from the drafting table and walked down the hallway. Tommy was right, he realized as he approached her. Attired casually in leggings, a hip-length T-shirt, and sandals, and with no hint of any makeup other than a subtle shade of pink lipstick, Mariah Chandler looked good enough to . . . He shuddered, the pressure in his groin intensifying, the muscles in his body coiling so tightly that he ached all over.

Jack paused in the doorway. "I don't have time for social calls."

"I'm not making one," Mariah replied as she sorted through the contents of her overflowing tote bag and produced a neatly folded document. "This is for you, Jack. It'll help you relax."

Relax, he thought grimly. He felt about as relaxed as a slab of concrete. Unfolding the legal-sized document, he skimmed it. He couldn't believe the contents of the typed page. He met Mariah's gaze and felt stunned by the gentle smile on her face. Steeling his emotions against her appeal, he gave her a steady look that said the proverbial ball was still in her court.

"I thought this might solve our problem."

"This doesn't solve a thing. You're still a civilian." He saw the determination that flashed in her eyes—eyes so blue that they reminded him of polished gemstones.

"Give a little, why don't you? You can afford to be gracious," she reminded him quietly. "This waiver of liability is ironclad. My attorney drew it up, but your attorney approved it and initialed it. He said to call him if you have any questions."

"Making your own rules again, Mariah?"

"Not at all. I'm just trying to meet your needs."

"My needs? Shall I give you a list of them, just so we'll both be clear about the situation?" His eyes narrowed, his thoughts on the sensual things he wanted to do to her and for her and with her.

"If you like," she answered, clearly unaware of the nature of his fantasies, "I'll attempt to do my best to meet them, provided, of course, my needs are also respected."

She doesn't have a clue about what she's doing to me, he realized suddenly. He hesitated.

On the other hand, maybe she did realize exactly what she was doing. "You're very thorough."

"I try to be. Meeting you halfway seems only fair."

She seemed to be trying to accommodate him, but why didn't that make him feel any better? Why couldn't he take her at face value and trust her? Simple. He'd trusted once before and had his life nearly ruined.

Something inside him lurched painfully. He remembered wanting Delia. Craving her like a drug he couldn't live without. She'd been his addiction, one he kept coming back to time and time again, until she'd finally done the unforgivable. His life destroyed and his pride shredded beyond recognition, he'd crawled away to lick his wounds and rebuild his life. Mariah forced him now to look back, and he loathed what he saw.

He wanted to loathe her, too, but as much as he tried, he kept failing. Was he that weak? he wondered. Or was she that clever?

It took Jack a moment, but he finally noticed her expectant expression as she peered up at him. He freed himself from his memories.

"Confine yourself to the first floor, and if you need anything, come to me. Clear?"

Mariah nodded. "Very clear. Thank you. I won't be any trouble."

He clamped his jaws together. He managed not to voice his opinion that the word trouble should be spelled M-A-R-I-A-H from now on.

She reached out and touched his arm, her voice faintly seductive in its softness. "I'll be careful."

Her fingers left what felt like scorch marks against his skin. His jaw hardened, and his dark eyes narrowed. "See that you are."

Mariah nodded and made her way into what had once been the drawing room of the mansion. Stripped bare of paint, wallpaper, and moldings, the spacious room contained a dozen floor-to-ceiling beveled-glass windows, two ornately carved oak mantels in desperate need of refinishing above extra-wide fireplaces, and almost as much floor space as a modestly sized home. Mariah deposited her tote bag in the center of the room. After tucking her thick braid beneath the cap she wore, she extracted a stack of wallpaper samples and a packet of paint chips from her bag.

Jack kept a close eye on her. He watched her compare color combinations like a pro, take measurements, and make notes on a pad she kept handy at all times. Her ability to concentrate surprised him, as did her consistently restrained demeanor.

Although he didn't feel at ease with her around, he found no fault with her behavior. He saw no evidence that she sought the attention of the ten men who worked for him, which surprised him even more. If anything, they found excuses to speak to her. One by one, they wandered into the drawing room and introduced themselves.

He gave her high marks for attending to her own business, although he doubted that her circumspect behavior would last very long. He remained wary and watchful, because she personified the kind of woman who attracted men with her quick smile and soft laughter. Easier on a man's eyes than she had any right to be, Mariah seemed unaware of her natural beauty.

His awareness of Mariah was a constant that he realized wouldn't end, and he knew he needed to find a way to deal with her. He promised himself that he would, but he sensed, down deep, that he was lying to himself. They were on a collision course that he doubted either one of them could avoid.

The crew finally broke for lunch. Jack overheard several of them invite Mariah to join them. She politely declined each invitation, but none of the men seemed offended. If anything, they easily accepted her lack of interest with good humor. Two of the men even offered to pick up a take-out meal for her, but she assured them that she wasn't hungry.

After inspecting the refurbished flooring in the formal dining room and marking the sections he felt needed additional sanding, Jack decided to take a break. "What the hell are you doing up there?" he barked when he walked by the drawing room and spotted Mariah perched atop a ladder.

She jerked in surprise, almost toppling the ladder. Her notebook and tape measure fell from her hands as she grabbed at a nearby wall to steady herself. His expression thunderous, Jack darted into the room and seized the ladder.

Wide-eyed, Mariah stared down at him. "What's wrong now?"

"You're what's wrong. Are you trying to break your neck?"

A smile broke across her face. Jack felt as though he were watching the sun burst to life at the start of a new day. It was the same smile that haunted his dreams and fueled his fantasies. It was that innocent smile that made him want her with a hunger that he knew could never be appeased, a seemingly innocent smile that made him want to take her and shake her until she came to her senses and stopped tormenting him with her lush figure and annoyingly resilient attitude.

"Answer me, damn it!"

She laughed, then smothered the sound behind her fingertips. "Of course not."

"Then what are you doing?"

"Studying the ceiling and the walls from a good vantage point. I can't decide whether to completely wallpaper this room, or paint it and then use a twelve-inch border just below the moldings once they're installed."

"You can't make that decision from down here?"

She glanced around. "It's a better perspective."

"It's also dangerous."

"Jack, for heaven's sake. I know what I'm doing. The only problem I really have is you. If you'd stop sneaking up on me, then I wouldn't always be dropping things."

"You don't know a damn thing. Get down from there."

She complied with his order, surprising him with her cooperation. He reached out for her when she paused at the halfway point of the ladder, unable to stop himself from seizing her by the waist and settling her on the floor in front of him. He didn't release her. Instead, his hold on her tightened. "Stay off that thing!"

"You aren't responsible for me."

"I'm responsible for everything that happens in this place." His fingers dug into her waist, and he jerked her forward so that her hips slammed into his loins. His response was instantaneous, and he didn't try to conceal it. Something flared in her eyes as she stared up at him, something hot and sultry that contrasted sharply with her innocent, all-American image. He felt her shiver, and he knew then that she would be the most responsive of lovers. He nearly groaned aloud, but he managed to quell the sound in time. He couldn't contain his craving for a taste of her, however.

Mariah tensed all over as he claimed her mouth. She relaxed, though, the instant he gentled his assault. He seduced her with his mouth, easily breaching the barrier of her lips. Cupping her hips, he brought her up and against the strength of his arousal and molded her to his aching loins. The jeans he wore did little to conceal his desire.

Mariah trembled and shimmied closer. Unwilling to question her responsiveness, Jack inhaled the faint moan that escaped her before delving beyond the boundary of her even teeth. She tasted sweet, so sweet that his body ached with the kind of need that provoked a man to do and say rash things in the heat of passion. He vowed not to do anything stupid, then realized that he'd already broken his vow.

Jack wanted to drown in her. He longed to submerge himself in the lushness of her body and in the wondrous flavors of her, but he restrained himself even after she angled her head and parted her lips for greater access. He felt her welcome the darting intrusion of his tongue. He jerked in surprise when she kissed him back, the tentative forays of the tip of her tongue sending ribbons of heat into his bloodstream before her inexperience hit him like a bolt of lightning. He lifted his head, his gaze dark and curious as he studied her flushed cheeks, dazed expression, and swollen mouth.

"Jack . . ." she began as she tried to shift free of him. She pushed at his hands, then seemed to sense the futility of her actions and stopped. "This isn't a good idea," she whispered.

He refused to allow her the freedom she sought, even after he lowered her so that she could regain her footing. He needed the contact, he realized. He felt her strain against his hold, but his instincts had taken over and wouldn't be denied quite yet. Hungry enough for her to discard his usual caution, he indulged in the silent battle of wills that ensued as she stared up at him.

Several minutes passed. Jack finally asked, "What's wrong, Mariah? Have you just realized that you've bitten off more than you can chew?"

"I realize," she said softly, "that something I don't understand is driving you. I realize that your body wants mine, even though your head is telling you that you must be nuts since you don't even like me. I realize that there's some kind of chemistry at work between us that neither one of us understands. I realize that it's easier for you to deal with me by putting me down, because then you don't have to confront your feelings, whatever they are. I realize, too, that you're trying to make me hate you, even though you know now that I'm attracted to you, but I don't." She hesitated, catching her breath as she searched his hard-featured face. "And I won't."

He abruptly freed her. "Why don't you go count paper clips or pencils at the foundation office? Isn't that what directors do while the staff does the real work?"

"You're impossible."

She started to turn away from him. Jack glimpsed the anger sparkling brightly in her large blue eyes. Grabbing her shoulder, he spun her around and forced her to meet his gaze once more.

"I'm careful, Mariah. Very careful."

She yanked her rumpled T-shirt into place. "Actually," she said, "you're wound tighter than an eight-day clock. Maybe you're hungry. Why don't you go get some lunch? You might feel better."

"I feel great," he lied.

"Do you? Well, you couldn't prove it by me."

She slipped past him by ducking out from under his hand. He didn't try to stop her. Mariah picked up the thermos that sat next to her tote bag. Opening the container, she poured a cup of iced tea with unsteady hands.

"Want some? I have an extra cup in here somewhere."

He saw the tremor in her hands. He felt a certain amount of satisfaction, because it matched the ones rippling through his muscular frame. "What I want I can't have," Jack muttered, furious with himself for wanting her, furious with her for tempting him.

"You're right. I don't intend to disappear," she announced, her misunderstanding of his comment apparent. "You'll get used to me. Your men already have." She walked to the window and peered out at the front yard.

As he watched her, Jack grudgingly admired her grit and grappled with his surprise that she'd willingly acknowledged the sexual sparks flying between them. Most women weren't as honest. He knew he'd never known one as strong as Mariah. He didn't know what to make of her, but he told himself that she wasn't worth the effort. The lie left a bitter aftertaste in his mouth.

She spoke so quietly a few minutes later that he strained to hear her. "I can't get over how peaceful it is here, even with all the work going on. It's so different from Washington."

"Most places are." He studied her through narrowed eyes. She looked small as she stood in front of the window, small and vulnerable and alone. Alone? Why had he applied that particular word to a woman like Mariah?

"You don't miss it at all, do you?"

Jack kept his voice even. "There's nothing to miss."

She glanced over her shoulder. "I'll tell you a secret that would probably astound most of the people who know me. I don't miss it either."

"Then why live there?"

"Foundation headquarters." She smiled faintly. "Lots of paper clips and pencils at that location."

He frowned at her self-deprecating tone. Like so many other things she said and did, it didn't fit the image he wanted to have of her.

"I'll be back tomorrow, and every day after that," she informed him, her stubborn nature much in evidence.

"Why doesn't that surprise me?"

She turned to look at him. "Unfortunately, I don't think much of anything surprises you."

"You're right," he ground out.

"You don't seem to get much joy out of life."

"Life is not a game."

"No, it's not, but it doesn't have to be a never-ending endurance test."

Jack shrugged, but it was obvious by the expression on his face that he knew she was right.

She took another sip of her tea. "Your crew's very nice."

"Most are family men."

She studied him as she finished her tea. Jack wondered what was going through her mind, but he didn't ask as she walked back to where she'd left her thermos.

Lifting it in invitation, she said, "Last chance."

Jack shook his head, his hands closing into fists at his sides. The loose top she wore failed to conceal the swell of her breasts. He'd already felt their bounty pressed against his chest. Now he wanted to touch them and feel their weight in his hands, the nipples tightening and stabbing into his palms. He swore suddenly, angry with himself, angrier still with her.

Looking unruffled despite the profane word he muttered, Mariah glanced at him after screwing on the cup to the thermos and depositing it in her tote bag. "I'm not here to seduce anyone, so discard that from your list of reasons to dislike me, why don't you? It'd be easier on all of us if you'd relax, so why don't you try thinking of me as part of the landscape."

"You mean like a thorny bush?"

She sighed. "Stubborn man, aren't you?"

"Only when necessary."

"Why did you kiss me?"

He countered instantly, "Why did you kiss me back?"

"I wanted to," she admitted. "You were very gentle. Both times. You surprised me. I'd . . . I'd still like to know why, Jack? What was the point? Are you the kind of man who notches his bedpost?"

Her reminder of their encounter in the elevator was unnecessary. He hadn't been able to forget it. As for his bedpost, he rarely took anyone to his home. He didn't indulge in sexual conquests. His home was his haven, and he felt reluctant to share it. "Conducting a survey?"

"What do you think?"

"*You* didn't surprise me," he said. In truth, she astounded him on so many levels and in so many ways that he couldn't keep track of them all.

Mariah exhaled softly. "I used to protect my emotions the way you do, but I learned not to waste my energy in such a negative manner. While you're very busy being cynical or afraid, you miss the goodness in people. For the record, I don't sleep around. Having high standards is an advantage in this day and age."

Slinging her tote bag over her shoulder, Mariah walked past him. She paused in the doorway, her normally sunny smile absent. "I'm doing everything in my power to be a good team player. Can't you give me a chance to fit in so that I can be a part of the restoration? It would mean a great deal to me, Jack."

"I kissed you because I craved the taste of you."

Mariah looked stunned by his bluntness, but she recovered quickly. "Thank you for being honest with me. I felt the same way, and I wasn't prepared for it."

Jack abruptly shifted gears. "Tell me why you wanted me to restore Chandler House." He saw the caution in her gaze the instant he made his demand.

"I've already told you. You're the best. I don't like settling for less."

As he watched her leave Jack felt a profound sense of shame. His conscience assured him that he'd been hard on Mariah, too hard, but he still didn't know how to come to terms with the emotional conflict she inspired. He doubted he ever would, despite how much he wanted her.

As the days and weeks unfolded, an unspoken truce emerged between Mariah and Jack. They warily skirted each other at first, speaking only when it was absolutely necessary. The crew looked on in amazement. Tommy made the observation that they had their own soap opera at the job site.

Mariah arrived early each morning, her behavior always restrained. Jack recognized the futility of chastising his men for spending time with her, but he couldn't stop himself from barking orders at her when he found her perched atop ladders or if she walked too close to a piece of dangerous machinery.

He knew his crew disapproved of his hard-nosed attitude, but he, in turn, found their easy acceptance of Mariah baffling. She did fit in, as she'd hoped to and in spite of him. She shook his presumption that everyone would eventually see that she lacked substance as a person and adaptability in an environment foreign to the one she normally inhabited.

He grew accustomed to her presence and found himself wondering about her when she wasn't underfoot. In spite of his determination to treat her as nothing more than the owner of the building he'd agreed to restore, Jack grew hungrier and hungrier for her with each passing day. Her fragrance teased him if he got too close to her. Her easy smile played havoc with his nerves. The shape of her body, especially when she wore shorts, sent his imagination into high speed and frayed his temper, which drew muffled laughter from his crew.

Because the men noticed his increasingly possessive attitude about Mariah, Jack felt torn between embarrassment that his desire for her had become so obvious and his relief that no one felt compelled to make a move on her. He discovered that he couldn't refrain from keeping a close watch over Mariah.

The crew included her in their conversations, as though wanting to ease the strain between their boss and the woman who had hired him. They treated her like a sister, taught her basic carpentry techniques, praised her brownies even though she scorched them more often than not, entertained her with amusing anecdotes from previous restoration projects, and shared family concerns with her.

Four weeks into the restoration, Jack overheard a conversation between Mariah and three of his crew late one Friday afternoon.

"I can't begin to thank you enough for volunteering your time at the shelter. I'll look for you all tomorrow morning. The lumber's been delivered already, and the bookshelves will be a wonderful addition to the center's family room."

Jack stepped aside as the men filed out of the upstairs bedroom. Looking somewhat uneasy, they hastily wished him a good weekend, descended the staircase, and began cleaning and securing their tools. They acted, he thought grimly, as though they felt he would disapprove of their volunteer spirit. Because Mariah lingered after their departure, Jack walked into the bedroom. Kneeling on the floor near the window, she was in the process of gathering up and stacking an array of lighting-fixture catalogs.

"What was that all about?" he asked.

When she paused and glanced at him, Jack saw the wariness in her eyes. He told himself he'd earned her caution, but it still gnawed at him.

"José, Mark, and Tommy volunteered to build bookshelves for us at Hazel Roth Center. They're coming over in the morning."

"This is only their second Saturday off in the last month. I wanted them to have time with their families."

"They volunteered. Mark and José will probably bring their children with them. They did the last time they helped us."

"I'm still surprised you'd ask them."

"I didn't ask them, Jack. They came to me, as hard as that might be for you to believe. I know their schedules, and I realize how much their families mean to them. I think they feel compassion for the women and children who use the shelter." She dusted her hands off as she got to her feet. Her fatigue showed in her features.

"You look tired."

A rueful sound escaped her. "Just what every woman wants to hear when she's already feeling kind of frazzled."

"What's the problem?"

"Nothing really. I just haven't gotten much sleep lately."

He imagined her in bed, a silky nightgown riding up her hips as she shifted restlessly atop the mattress. His insides clenched and coiled in response. He wanted to share her bed and her nights. He wanted to know what it felt like to sink slowly into the heat of her body and abandon himself in the passion he felt certain he would find with her. Jack's voice sounded rough when he remarked, "Sounds like you need to tone down your social life."

She flashed a bright smile in his direction. "You're probably right."

"I'm not, am I?"

"No, you're not. I'm glad you realize it."

Jack glanced at his watch. "Can I drop you at your place?"

"Thanks, but José has already offered. He's probably waiting for me now."

"Get some rest. Fatigue can cause accidents on the job." *Great!* he thought in disgust. *Now you sound like her parent.*

She nodded as she walked into the hallway. "Have we reached the point yet that we can declare a formal truce?" Mariah asked.

Because this wasn't the first time she'd asked him that question, Jack decided to let down his guard and meet her halfway. "We have a formal truce," he said, his gaze locked on her face as he watched her reaction.

Although startled, Mariah was obviously relieved. "I'm glad, Jack. I'm very glad."

They ended the day on that note, both hesitant to believe the step they'd just taken, both hopeful that their official truce could be maintained.

FIVE

A few weeks later, as Mariah conferred with the subcontractor Jack had chosen to handle the kitchen and bathroom tile installation, she suddenly heard a man's voice echo down the hallway. Her blood froze in her veins. The man sounded sober, but that hadn't been the case two nights earlier when he'd tried to assault his wife after breaking into the shelter.

Mariah had spent that night as she did two nights each week—as an on-call driver between the police station and the local foundation-sponsored shelter for battered women and their children. Richard Hilton had shown up at the facility in defiance of instructions given by the police officers who intervened in cases of domestic violence. Mariah had summoned the police to have him removed from the center once the volunteers on duty had trapped the drunken man in a broom closet.

Mariah remembered hearing that he was an electrician by trade, but it hadn't occurred to her until now that he might be one of the sub-contractors employed by Jack. She also grimly recalled Hilton's threats to anyone who challenged his authority over his wife and children as the police had led him out of the shelter to a waiting police vehicle. She then recalled his specific threat that *she* would regret interfering in his private business. She knew from experience that men like Hilton often carried out their threats. And like Hilton, they rarely spent more than a night or two in jail before posting bail. Instead of feeling any emotion akin to remorse, they feverishly plotted their revenge.

Mariah thought about the stun gun in her purse. Her grandmother had given it to her, and she automatically carried it with her, though she'd never needed it. It was a potential way of defending herself if Richard Hilton came at her.

Not that she wanted a confrontation with the hostile-natured man here and now at the mansion. The formal truce she'd forged with Jack was still fragile, and she didn't want it disturbed. Neither did she wish to place him or his crew in the middle of a dispute between herself and a disgruntled abuser. Needing time to think through a solution to the situation, Mariah settled on a temporary course of action.

"Miss Chandler?"

Startled from her thoughts, Mariah redirected her gaze to the round-faced tile contractor. "I'm sorry, Mr. Shaw. What were you saying?"

"I think we've covered everything for now. I'll let Jack know we've completed the selection process, and I'll place the order today. Since the manufacturer is located in Los Angeles, it shouldn't take more than a week or so to receive the tile and grouting compounds."

"Thank you. You've been very patient with me this morning. Perhaps you'll allow me to observe when your installers are working."

Shaw doffed his baseball cap and smiled. "It'll be our pleasure, miss."

Mariah kept her expression even as she listened to the sound of Richard Hilton's voice and watched Shaw gather up his tile samples. Hilton was moving down the hallway, she realized. Her desire increased to avoid becoming engaged in a nasty scene with the man, which could be the only result once he recognized her as the architect of his obviously brief stay in the local jail, as well as the person who'd signed the request that a restraining order be issued against him.

While she didn't doubt that the crew, if

informed of Hilton's violent proclivities, would defend her, she preferred not to put them in the position of having to do so. Nor did she want to provoke Hilton into making another midnight raid on the shelter. She sensed that her best option for dealing with him was not to deal with him at all unless she was testifying against him on behalf of his wife in a court of law.

Mariah reached for her purse, slipped on her sunglasses, and said good-bye to the tile contractor. Walking out the backdoor just as Hilton and two members of Jack's crew strolled into the kitchen, she made her way around to the front of the mansion. Mariah passed a dusty van that said HILTON ELECTRICAL SERVICES, a shudder moving through her as she thought again about the man's three victims. She set out down the narrow winding road that led to the gardener's cottage, but she paused and turned when she heard a familiar and far more appealing voice.

"Quitting for the day, Vassar?" Jack asked as he approached her.

She caught her breath as she looked at him. Clad in age-softened jeans that were almost bleached white, his ever-present cowboy boots, and a teal-colored T-shirt that did nothing to conceal the muscular strength of his chest, Jack reminded her of the darkly dangerous male models so popular now in fashion magazines.

"Cat got your tongue?"

She shook her head. "I . . . missed lunch." Mariah disliked lying to Jack, but she was determined not to entangle him in the business of the shelter.

"I'll walk along with you. I need to stretch my legs."

"All right."

"You look pale," he remarked as he adapted his long-legged stride to match hers.

"No makeup. I look like a ghost without it."

Jack frowned. "Something's bothering you. What is it?"

"Nothing, really. I'm just hungry. I overslept this morning and didn't have time to pack a lunch."

"Would you rather be by yourself?"

Mariah glanced up at him, thankful that he cared enough to ask. She prayed that her conflicted emotions didn't show, but she suspected they did. "I'd prefer your company to my own."

Jack simply nodded. They walked the short distance to the cottage in companionable silence. Mariah felt the force of his curiosity in his repeated glances, and she appreciated his restraint when he didn't press her for a more thorough explanation of her behavior.

They paused on the flagstone steps at the front door of the cottage. Mariah dug through her purse, found her keys, and unlocked both the dead bolt and the door. She looked up at Jack, aware that he seemed reluctant to leave. She wanted his company, and after a small inner war that took all of ten seconds to resolve, she said as much. "José brought me some tomatoes from his garden yesterday. I thought I'd make a club sandwich. If you'd like to join me, I have plenty of ingredients for a second sandwich."

Looking pensive, he pondered her proposal, then asked, "How about a third, perhaps even a fourth? I worked up a major appetite this morning."

Mariah smiled at the teasing note in his voice. Her tension eased, and she felt unexpectedly relaxed and happy as she responded to his playful mood. "I think that can be arranged."

"Then I'll stay. José's tomatoes are legendary. He must have given you the ones he usually brings to me. I'll have to have a chat with him, since this is a clear violation of his employment contract."

She laughed. "Then I'm more than willing to share. He provided me with a lifetime supply after dropping a bushel-basketful at the shelter."

"I'll hold you to that," he said as he followed her into the sun-drenched interior of her temporary home.

Mariah set aside her purse and sunglasses

as Jack paused just inside the front door of the cottage, which resembled a sprawling studio apartment. She noticed the way his gaze swept the rectangular-shaped room, his thickly lashed hazel eyes widening with unconcealed amazement when he spotted the gauze-draped iron-frame bed situated to the right of the floor-to-ceiling front windows.

Amused, Mariah watched him take note of the pale mauve satin bedding, the elaborate cream-colored netting that made the bed look like something from an exotic movie set, and the jumble of mauve satin pillows clustered at the head of the bed. A cream-colored leather love seat and a carved teak coffee table situated atop an area rug filled the other half of the room, while the small kitchen that extended along half of the back wall of the cottage boasted the basic appliances found in most homes and a bar with two stools. The bathroom, dressing room, and a walk-in closet were situated behind a set of French doors.

"Interesting," he finally said as he looked at her.

"Cozy and multipurpose. I don't need a lot of space. I'm used to hotel suites, so this actually feels quite roomy." She smiled and gestured in the direction of the love seat. "Make yourself comfortable."

"I will."

As Jack wandered around the cottage and then paused to inspect the contents of the bookcase built into a small alcove that also contained a desk and chair, Mariah arranged the sandwich ingredients on a breadboard. After pulling a bag of potato chips from one of the cupboards and placing it on the bar, she glanced up to find Jack studying the assembly line of ingredients.

"Very organized."

She grinned. "You've discovered my fatal flaw. I'm always trying to make order out of chaos."

"Need any help?" he asked, a hint of a smile lifting the edges of his mouth.

Mariah felt her heartbeat speed up. She loved his smile, because in it she saw both his sensuality and his humanity. She also thought she saw the beginning of trust and friendship, but she cautioned herself against expecting too much, too soon from Jackson McMillan Wainright III. He was a man who vigilantly guarded his turf.

"Mariah?"

She nodded, embarrassed to have been caught staring at him. "Please. We'll need a platter, plates, napkins, and glasses. They're all located beneath the bar. You can pour the iced tea while I toast the bread."

"Sounds like a deal."

She realized then that she'd never seen him this relaxed. Relief flooded her and renewed optimism surged to life inside her heart. This was the man who'd been hidden behind hostility and suspicion. While she would have liked to have known the reason for his antipathy at the start of their relationship, Mariah sensed that she'd finally been accepted as an integral part of the restoration process. She refused to question her good fortune.

Jack's temper rarely surfaced now. When it did, she knew it was the result of his intolerance for slipshod workmanship by subcontractors. The structural renovation of the mansion was nearly complete, the interior rooms reframed, the exterior walls reinforced, a new roof in place, and the fireplaces rebricked. Once all the wiring was redone, Sheetrock would be bolted into place for the sake of structural soundness in earthquake-prone Southern California.

Her smile faded as she considered the possibility that Richard Hilton would be the electrician who would handle the wiring. A part of her derived a certain amount of pleasure from the idea that he would unknowingly help to create an environment that would benefit women and children who'd fled men like him, while another part of her, the practical side, made her realize that she would have to avoid the mansion as long as he worked there.

"Talk to me, Mariah."

She jerked in surprise. "Pardon me?"

"You're a thousand miles away. Am I such miserable company?"

She flushed and busied herself at the toaster. "I was just thinking about one of the upstairs bedrooms."

"No, you weren't. What's got you so rattled?"

"I'm all right," she insisted as she turned to face him. "Just a little preoccupied."

She deftly assembled four thick club sandwiches and arranged them on the platter under his skeptical gaze. They seated themselves on the stools and ate in silence. Jack polished off three sandwiches, half the bag of chips, and two full glasses of iced tea. Mariah picked at her food, drawing a frown and finally the comment that she had the eating habits of a bird. She saw no point in contradicting the obvious accuracy of his observation.

After clearing their dishes and placing a plate of brownies in front of Jack, she urged, "Tell me about your childhood."

Jack looked surprised. "There's not much to tell."

"You grew up in Virginia, didn't you?"

He nodded as he took a bite from a brownie.

"Were you an only child?

"Yes."

"Me too. I missed having brothers and sisters. Did you?"

"It can get lonely," he conceded. "But children are adaptable, and I was no exception."

"Were your parents attentive?" she asked, her voice faint as she recalled her own self-indulgent mother and father.

"Above average in that department, I suspect. They made time for me, and I knew I could count on them not to park me in a boarding school and forget me. A lot of my friends weren't as fortunate. How about you?"

"Boarding schools started in first grade, but I preferred it that way, especially after my parents died."

Clearly surprised by her admission, he asked, "Why?"

"Too many relatives trying to use me as a tennis ball in their never-ending match to see who would be given control over my inheritance, but my grandmother discovered what was going on, stepped in, and petitioned for custody. She helped me regain my emotional balance."

"Sounds like a nice lady."

As she sat there Mariah recalled both her tumultuous childhood and her marriage to Darren. Emma Lacey Chandler had ridden to her rescue both times. Mariah knew she owed her grandmother far more than a building with her name on it; she owed her her sanity and her life. "She saved me. More than once."

Settled comfortably against the wall behind his bar stool, Jack studied her. "Are you sure you're all right? You're not acting like yourself, and you still look too pale."

"I'll be fine."

"You should eat more."

"I usually do." She smiled gently. "I take my vitamins every morning, so there's no need to worry about me. Scout's honor."

"Something's bothering you," he said firmly.

"How can you tell?"

"You refuse to look me in the eye when I ask a question you don't want to answer. You're usually more confrontational and far more animated."

Mariah tried to lighten his mood as she forced a smile to her lips. "Sounds like you know me fairly well."

"I should by now, don't you think?"

"Does that mean," she said, "you've finally realized that I'm not an ax murderer?"

He shrugged and ignored her attempt at levity. "I haven't seen you this subdued since you tiptoed around me those first weeks at the mansion."

"You gave me good reason not to draw your attention. You yelled at me every hour on the hour for that first month. I was giving serious thought to investing in earplugs."

He exhaled, the sound harsh. "I should probably apologize."

She grinned, unable to help herself as she took in the extent of his discomfort with his own behavior. "I'd faint dead away if you did, Jack McMillan."

He shook his head, his expression dubious as he set aside his napkin and slid off his stool. "If you decide you want to talk, I'll listen. If one of the crew's gotten out of line, I expect you to tell me."

"I don't have anything to talk about, they haven't done anything but treat me with affection and kindness. The edge in your voice could slice through granite, and my hearing is excellent. Would you like a note from my doctor?"

"Now you sound like the Mariah Chandler I know."

She groaned. "Look, I'm just tired, that's all. I need a nap and a long soak in a hot tub."

Jack moved forward, slipping between her parted legs. Mariah felt the heat he generated and the heat that flowed through her veins. Mariah held very still as he cupped her face between his hands. She stared up at him, the air moving unevenly in and out of her body.

"You in a bathtub is a very seductive image."

Her eyes widened. "If you say so."

"I say so, Vassar." He studied her, his eyes dark and stormy looking. "No one's made a move on you?"

"No one." She swallowed, and her voice regained its strength. "It's not going to happen, Jack, so quit expecting the worst."

"You sound very certain. Tommy overestimates his charm at times, and Jim thinks he's nature's answer to the women of Santa Barbara. They're both capable of poor judgment."

"They treat me like an older sister, and I always treat them like younger brothers. I trust the men who work for you, because they've earned my trust. I have fairly good instincts about people, better than you can even begin to imagine about certain types of men. I know which ones to avoid."

He traced the fullness of her lower lip with his thumb, then asked in a low voice, "And what do your instincts tell you about me?"

She caught her breath as she tried to deal with the sensations his light touch evoked. "A lot. You don't trust easily, but when you do, you'll stand beside a friend to the bitter end if you believe he needs your help and support."

Looking doubtful, he remarked, "I'm hardly that noble, and I seriously doubt that my character is quite that sterling. Tarnish my image a bit, and you'll find the real me."

"I don't agree. I've seen you under pressure. The men who work for you idolize you. They also respect you, and they care about you. You, in turn, consider their needs as human beings. You don't just employ them. You're their role model, as a man and as a restorer. You've earned their loyalty, primarily because you give it back to them tenfold and they know it."

Jack looked shocked. "You seem to have forgotten my lousy temper."

"You control it, and that separates you from people who behave like primates most of the time."

"You sound like an expert on the subject, but then being the director of the Chandler Foundation probably helps," he speculated as he released her and stepped back.

She immediately missed his closeness and his touch. "It does. When I'm not counting paper clips and pencils, I read the literature on domestic violence, so I know more about it than most people ever really want to know."

He leaned back against the bar, his hands jammed into the front pockets of his jeans. The fabric emphasized his maleness, his narrow hips, and the muscular strength of his thighs.

"How'd the bookshelves at the shelter turn out?"

Mariah smiled, grateful for a distraction. "Just wonderful. José and Tommy let the children help paint once the shelves were installed. Did you know that José's wife volunteers one afternoon a week in the play yard now?"

"They're goodhearted people."

"She likes you too," Mariah said with a gentle smile. "She does think you're a bit excessive in the macho department, though."

"Then I'll have to try to be less macho, won't I?"

"I don't think anyone wants you to change, Jack." She paused, then said, "José told me what you're doing for their eldest boy."

Jack shrugged. "He's a bright kid. Helping him with his tuition makes sense."

"He wants to be an architect."

"So they tell me."

"Don't you miss it?" she asked.

"I use the skills, but in different ways now. I'm content, Mariah, so don't read anything into the choices I made ten years ago."

"You're professionally content as a restorer?"

"I'm content." He spoke in a tone of voice that didn't invite any more questions on the topic.

Mariah sensed his need to change the subject

and responded to it. "Our truce seems to be working."

"How do you feel about that, Vassar?"

"Relieved." She glanced past him, her gaze snagging for a long moment on the iron-frame bed across the room. "I meant it when I told you I liked you."

"If I hadn't eased up on you, my crew would have mutinied."

She laughed. "I seriously doubt that."

"I don't doubt it for a minute. Are you happy with the progress we're making at the mansion?"

"Very happy. You're ahead of schedule, aren't you?"

"By about a week or so. The men seem to understand your passion for the place."

Her humor faded as she studied his strongly boned features. "But you don't, do you?"

"Let's put it this way," he said. "I'd still like to know the real reason behind your commitment and dedication. I'd also like to know how Darren figures into the situation."

Mariah stiffened. Mention of Darren was like being struck across the face without any warning. "He has nothing to do with me or my life. Restoring Chandler House is my way of paying tribute to my grandmother. As you observed a few minutes ago, she was a very nice lady."

"She's just part of it, Mariah. I'm not a complete fool, you know. Something else is driving you. I'll eventually figure it out."

Startled, she insisted, "I've never thought of you as a fool, just amazingly muleheaded about certain things."

"Then tell me who or what upset you this afternoon," he urged once more.

"Jack, please don't push me. If I have a problem, I'll resolve it."

"You're lying." Crossing the room, he opened the front door. He turned and asked, "Are you coming back to the mansion this afternoon?"

"I don't think so."

"Then I'll see you tomorrow."

Mariah seriously doubted that they would see each other for several days. She slid off her stool and hurried to the doorway. Thanks to José, she already knew that the rewiring of the mansion would take at least a week.

She lingered in the open doorway until Jack disappeared from sight. She would miss him, but she couldn't and wouldn't alter her commitments, regardless of how deeply she cared for him.

SIX

Mariah summoned her patience and stayed away from the mansion for several days. She photographed the daily progress of the restoration early each morning before Jack and his crew arrived, accomplishing one of the goals she'd set for herself while still eliminating a confrontation with Richard Hilton.

She missed being a part of the mansion's transformation, but she stayed busy by catching up on Chandler Foundation correspondence. She also rented a storage facility for the furniture being amassed for eventual placement in the mansion, and she made last-minute calls to prospective contributors to encourage their participation in a fund-raising event scheduled for the coming weekend in Montecito, a community adjacent to Santa Barbara and known for its philanthropic residents and close ties to Hollywood.

Mariah devoted countless hours to coming to terms with her growing feelings for Jack. She realized that she cared more for him than she had for any man she'd ever known. He inspired within her heart the fledgling hope of one day being loved and desired for herself. He occupied her thoughts day and night, astoundingly erotic images drifting through her mind at unexpected moments.

For the first time since her disastrous marriage to Jack's stepbrother, Mariah sensed the need finally to free emotions kept under lock and key for the previous five years. She still felt cautious about making herself vulnerable emotionally. Even though she'd suffered both mentally and physically at Darren's hands, she trusted the integrity and honor intrinsic to Jack's nature.

He was by turns compassionate and demanding, insightful and relentless, overprotective and fiercely independent. He also possessed the ability to read her emotions, which often startled her. While Mariah felt anxious about the possibility of rejection at Jack's hands, she knew that she would respond if he chose to move beyond the boundaries he'd established between them. She sensed without a doubt that Jack would be a sensitive lover.

Mariah longed to know him in every way

that a woman could know a man. She wanted his tenderness and the passion simmering beneath his surface. She wanted to understand the reasons for his self-protectiveness. She wanted to feel free to express those parts of herself that had been muted by a damaging marriage. Her personal history repeatedly assured her that Jack had been badly hurt at some point in the past, and she prayed that he would relinquish his pain and lower the barriers around his heart in order to be loved again.

Mariah developed a case of cabin fever following a week of self-imposed isolation. Too restless to remain indoors for another evening, she decided to stroll to the mansion. She carried a flashlight to illuminate the rutted road. As she approached the three-story dwelling she hesitated when she spotted Jack's truck parked in the otherwise vacant front yard.

She missed him so much that she couldn't bring herself to ignore an opportunity to see him. Shelving her pride, Mariah trusted her instincts as she made her way inside. She found Jack leaning over the drafting table that sat beneath a temporary light fixture in the formal drawing room.

The sound of her footsteps alerted him to her presence. He straightened and turned to look at her before she could speak, the cynical expression on his face making her smile of greeting fade.

Mariah knew instantly that she'd overestimated her own charm. "You're obviously busy. I'll leave you to your work."

"Been out of town, Vassar?" The whiplash sharpness of his voice matched the tension vibrating through his muscular body. Clad in scuffed boots, jeans, and a matching denim shirt open at the throat and the sleeves rolled up to reveal his tanned forearms, he looked powerful, sexy, and thoroughly irritated.

Mariah took a step backward into the hallway, not out of cowardice, but out of a need to preserve the rapport they'd managed to forge. "I'll see you later, Jack, when you're in a friendlier mood."

"I guess you've finally gotten bored with all of this, haven't you?"

She lifted her chin. "I've been busy."

"Doing what?"

She deliberately hedged. "Several different things, as a matter of fact."

"Try again, Mariah."

She understood his demand for an explanation of her absence during the previous week. Jack the Dictator was back, she realized. Mariah shifted her gaze away from his face, feeling guilty even before she spoke. "Haven't you ever heard of scheduling conflicts?"

"Be honest enough to admit the truth. Your interest in the restoration is waning, and you've moved on to other conquests."

Something in his tone of voice, coupled with his use of a word like *conquests*, made her wonder if he was even angry with her at all. Although she didn't feel inclined to delude herself, Mariah couldn't help wondering if his anger was based on the fact that he'd missed her. She secretly hoped so.

Mariah fought the urge to tell him the truth about Richard Hilton. She knew that any explanation, no matter how cursory, held the potential of spawning other truths. Truths she felt reluctant to reveal at this point about her past and her marriage to Darren. Even if she spoke in general terms about spousal abuse, she suspected that Jack would connect her passion for the subject to personal experiences. She couldn't handle that just yet with any man—not even Jack, whom she trusted even when his temper unraveled.

After taking a steadying breath, Mariah crossed the room. She approached him with a determined look on her face. Taking one of his hands, she clasped it between her own and gently stroked his skin.

"I'm waiting, Mariah."

"Restoring Chandler House is more important to me than you seem to realize. I think about it every single day, but I have other responsibilities that I can't ignore." As she studied him she saw some of his tension start to ease from his features. "You look worn-out. Why are you working so late?" His stunned expression told her that her concern startled him, and she wondered why. Hadn't anyone taken the time to treat him with gentleness and compassion in recent years?

"I lost track of time," he admitted, his voice subdued.

"That happens to me a lot too."

Jack nearly smiled. "Counting paper clips is demanding work."

"Somebody's got to do it," She quipped.

"Thanks. I owe you."

"For what?"

"For not clawing my eyes out a few minutes ago. I wouldn't have faulted you if you had."

Withdrawing her hands, she glanced meaningfully at her shorter-than-usual fingernails. "You'd have been disappointed, I'm afraid. I'm just glad my manicurist can't see the condition of my nails right now. I've been rendered clawless."

Jack slipped his arm around her shoulders and nudged her forward to the drafting table. "What do you think of the plans for the gazebo? I thought I'd have José center it in the old rose garden, then have the landscaper work around it."

Mariah smiled, savoring their closeness and the sturdy feel of his body as she perused his proposed sketch for a latticed gazebo. "It's wonderful. My impression from the watercolor prints done of the old rose garden was that it lacked a focal point. I think you've designed the perfect solution."

He nodded, his gaze still faintly critical as he scanned the sketch once more. "I'm finally satisfied with it."

She glanced at him, acutely aware of his physical prowess and the musky scent of his skin. "You demand a great deal of yourself."

"Too few people place enough emphasis on high standards."

"It's more than that with you, I suspect. I get the feeling that you're consciously creating a professional legacy."

"You mean rather than a personal one?"

She nodded.

He exhaled heavily. "You may be right."

"I can't help wondering why," Mariah admitted.

He lifted his free hand to his neck and massaged the back of it. "It's complicated."

"I gathered as much."

Jack met her gaze, unexpected vulnerability shining in his dark eyes until he blinked and looked away. "I can't talk about it."

"If you ever change your mind, I'm a good listener."

"You're more than that, Mariah Chandler. Much more."

She smiled. "Is that good or bad?"

He hesitated for several moments before answering. "I'm not sure."

"I noticed the banisters on my way in," she said, changing the subject for both their sakes. "I can't even begin to imagine the hours of work that must have gone into them."

"I've been working on them in my spare time."

Mariah shifted within the circle of his arm, her hip brushing against him as she turned to face him. She felt his arousal, and it fueled her own desire for him.

"They're . . . gorgeous, Jack," she managed to say as her heart rate increased and all the pulse points in her body throbbed. "At the risk of repeating myself, you're a gifted restorer. Chandler House is lucky to have you."

"Why won't you trust me?" he asked quietly.

"I do, probably more than you realize."

"Then why are you hiding out in the gardener's cottage like a criminal? Why the change in your routine?"

"I had a lot of paper clips to count. Pencils too," she teased.

Jack muttered a word that should have made her recoil, but the whispered softness of it aroused her instead, aroused her so quickly that when he breathed the word a second time, leaned down, and took her lips, Mariah sank against him and willingly surrendered to the seductive quality of his kiss.

His hands came up to frame her face as he angled his head for more thorough access. She eagerly parted her lips. He laved her sensitive inner lip with the tip of his tongue before delving deeply into her mouth.

Mariah felt flames burst to life inside her—flames that healed instead of destroyed, flames that made her dizzy from the depth of the hunger they incited in her soul, flames that enhanced her sense of herself as a woman. She welcomed them, just as she welcomed his taste and the thrusting intimacy of his tongue.

She brought her hands up to his chest, her fingertips kneading, seeking, learning, and then memorizing the feel of the flexing muscles that rippled beneath her touch. She dug her short nails into the fabric of his shirt, frustrated by the barrier.

Jack sucked at her mouth like a man desperate for nourishment. She answered every deft stroke of his tongue with one of her own, her hunger for him unleashed, her desire blinding her to the fact that they were standing in the middle of an empty room in an unfinished home.

She cared little for reality at that moment. She felt reckless and free and conscious of nothing but Jack, the hard wall of his chest, the darkly exotic flavors of his mouth, and the possessive grip of his hands at her shoulders. Fumbling with the buttons of his shirt, she silently cursed her own clumsiness until she parted the fabric and drove her fingers into the dense hair that covered his chest.

He groaned, shuddering beneath her touch. He held her close, his arms circling her shoulders as though fearful that she might decide to flee. Mariah moaned into his mouth as the seductive heat and power of him sent renewed sensation swirling into her bloodstream.

Breathless, heart-pounding wonder swamped her. She trembled with awe and yearned for even more. She'd never known or experienced true passion, but she wanted it. Craved it. Now. With Jack.

She murmured his name like a chant as he ate at her lips, but he silenced her a moment later as he deepened their kiss yet again. She felt the barely restrained power of his body when he ran his hands down her narrow back and past her waist, curved them over her hips, and snugged her into the V of his muscular legs.

Their intimate alignment allowed Mariah to experience the full extent of the hard flesh pressing against her pelvis. She longed to take him into her body for a slow, scintillating journey to fruition, but his drugging kiss prevented her from speaking.

The strength of his desire, not just the heightened sensations streaming through her entire body as he sensuously rocked against her, elicited a raw, mewling sound of urgency from Mariah. She clutched at his shoulders, shaken to her core by the energy and need flowing through her veins.

She knew then that Jack possessed the power to erase her memories of violence with new memories of generous, mutually satisfying passion. He'd already eased the loneliness that had haunted her for so many years. As much as she wanted him, her inexperience made her uncertain about how to tell him, how to express the extent of her desire for him. She attempted to convey her feelings as she slipped her arms around his waist, pressed her fingers against the base of his spine, and returned his openmouthed kiss with a searching, scorching foray of her own.

Jack jerked his mouth free a few minutes later, a growl of frustration bursting from him. Lifting her up with ease, he wrapped her legs around his hips with shaking hands and carried her across the room. He pressed her back against the unpainted Sheetrock wall and stared down at her. His breathing remained ragged, his eyes heavy-lidded, and ruddy color stained his hard cheeks.

"What's wrong?" she gasped.

Without warning, he drove his hard loins against her aching femininity as he framed her face with his callused palms and threaded his narrow fingers through her thick, pale hair. "I cannot believe what you do to me," he said, his voice hoarse and low.

"I've never felt ... I don't ..." Her voice trailed off. She exhaled, the sound catching and becoming a half sob. Determined to control herself, Mariah bit down on her lower lip, but a tremor of sensation worked its way from the tip of her toes to the top of her head anyway.

Jack placed a fingertip against her lips. "Don't even try to talk, Vassar. Words don't exist for what's happening between us. Just let yourself feel."

Shaking with desire, Mariah felt emotionally raw. Tears threatened to choke her, but she swallowed against them. "I want you," she whispered brokenly as she ignored his advice. "I want you so much I ache from it. I didn't know I could feel this way."

Jack inhaled sharply. Mariah felt the surging

force of his maleness as it strained against the fit of his jeans. Reverting to instinct, she sucked the fingertip gently tracing the width of her lower lip into her mouth, teased it with gentle teeth, and then swirled her tongue around it. She watched him the entire time, watched the surprise that flashed in his face, watched the way his eyes fell closed for several moments.

"Touch me, please," Mariah finally said, her voice soft and vulnerable, her need for him too acute to ignore. "I want to feel your hands on my skin."

His eyes darkened even more. She saw the heat that flared in them, and she felt it when his mouth settled over hers and his fingertips skimmed across her midriff beneath the cotton top she wore, leaving hot streaks in their wake. She trembled, then found the courage to guide his hands up to her breasts and hold them against her sensitive flesh.

He cupped her, his thumbs flicking at her nipples until she wanted to scream from the pleasure he gave her, but then his hands shifted. Before she could react, he separated their mouths, lifted his head while simultaneously seizing the hem of her top, and stripped it off her body.

Naked from the waist up, Mariah leaned her head back against the wall and caught her breath. Her back arched, her plump breasts swayed gently, her nipples distended peaks that invited his attention. She made no effort to conceal herself from his view. She wanted him to see her, needed him to touch her again.

Jack's gaze fell from her passion-flushed face to her exposed breasts, his hands shaking as he caressed her. "You're exquisite, Mariah. Your skin's like burning silk."

He shifted her higher, his lips and tongue torturing her with breath-stopping sensations as he sucked and nipped at her breasts. He paid special attention to her nipples, teething her until she moaned. She dug her fingers into his shoulders. He became her entire focus. Time seemed suspended. Awash in an ocean of sensuality, Mariah surrendered completely to the feelings and emotions flowing through her.

Jack eased her down, then reclaimed her mouth. His fingertips skimmed back and forth over her breasts, testing, teasing, and tantalizing her senses. He tugged at the coral buds until Mariah thought she would die from the glorious sensations cascading through her body. Never, she realized, not even in her wildest dreams, had she imagined the existence of this kind of mutual passion and sensual bonding between a man and a woman.

She tangled her tongue with Jack's, a seductive duel ensuing. His body tightened until he reminded Mariah of a length of hot coiled steel. A harsh sound escaped him as he raised his head. She couldn't stop the sound of protest that slid past her lips. Peering at him from beneath partially lowered lashes, she felt dazed and disoriented.

He raised and pressed his fists to both sides of the wall above her head, trapping her between his tall, muscular body and the wall. She kept her arms around his waist, her legs too unstable to keep her upright without help. She struggled to tame the sensations flooding her body as she leaned her forehead against his shoulder and closed her eyes. She sighed, the sound ripe with frustration. Unable to quell the impulse to touch him once more, she trailed the backs of her hands up his thighs to his loins.

Jack straightened abruptly and grabbed her wrists. "Don't!"

Stunned, she stared at him. Mariah felt her heart begin to shrivel. Wrenching free, she quickly crossed her arms over her breasts.

"We can't do this, Mariah."

His words felt like a body blow. He didn't want her. Her pride devastated, she nodded, ducked past him before he could stop her, and picked up her top from the floor. As she straightened, Jack took hold of her shoulders and gently tugged her back against his still-aroused body. She felt his strength as his arms circled around her. He held her in place despite her struggle to free herself.

"Stop fighting me, Vassar. You don't understand what you're doing to me."

She didn't hear his words, just the sound of her own heartbeat as it roared in her ears. She felt rejected, empty, and humiliated. She wanted to run and hide, the desire to protect herself expanding within her with every passing second. It was an all too familiar feeling, and she hated it.

"I asked you to trust me," he reminded her, his voice still ragged.

"I did."

"You still can," he vowed.

He turned her around in spite of the rigid set of her shoulders and the emotional pain that stiffened her slender body. A tear slipped free of her brimming eyes, then another.

"You feel everything more deeply than most people, don't you?" Jack leaned down, licking away each droplet that slid down her cheeks. He left a trail of kisses in his wake.

His tenderness made her feel even worse. "I don't need your pity. If you don't want me, then please just say so. But don't play with me. It's cruel." Her voice splintered.

"Look at me, Mariah."

She did as he asked, but very reluctantly. He took her hand and placed it over the front of his jeans. Her fingers curled of their own accord over the pulsing strength of his manhood.

Jack grimaced at her intimate touch, then ground his jaws together and steadied himself before he said, "I still want you. I've wanted you since the very beginning. I think I'll always want you."

Stroking him, she insisted, "I want you too."

He shook his head. "No."

Emboldened by her own needs, Mariah refused to accept an edict from Jack. She expected an explanation. "Why not?"

He glanced meaningfully around the room. "It's not the right time or the right place. You deserve better than this. You also deserve to be protected, and I can't do that right now."

"And I can't protect myself," she admitted, clearheaded and chagrined with herself now that she comprehended his restraint and the reason for it. She felt like a fool for not thinking about the need for birth control, but she knew she could put his mind to rest about another important issue. "I haven't been with anyone since . . . in several years. I'm healthy."

Jack nodded his understanding. "I haven't either, and my last physical was very thorough. You have nothing to worry about with me."

"I trust you, Jack. I always have, even when you were trying to run me off." She smiled, then deliberately flexed her newly found confidence with her next remark. "You want me."

His hold on her tightened. "More than I want to breathe," he said in a rough, low voice that aroused her all over again. "We'll find the right time, Vassar. Trust me on that, all right?"

Her gentle smile widened to a grin. "Only if you promise to keep breathing. It'll be more fun for both of us that way."

Jack pretended to scowl at her as he took her cotton top and helped her put it on, but Mariah knew he wasn't annoyed with her. After he smoothed the wrinkled fabric into place, his hands lingered at her breasts. She felt the faint tremors that moved through his fingers. Corresponding streamers of pleasure unfurled inside her yet again. "I love it when you touch me."

He pulled his hands away as though she were a temptation he doubted he could resist and worked on the buttons of his own shirt. "I love touching you."

"I'm glad."

He chuckled, but the sound rustled like old newspapers and lacked any real humor. "Very little surprises me as a general rule, but you surprised me tonight."

Mariah flushed. "I'm not very good at this."

Jack nodded, his features sober, thoughtful. "I believe you."

"Ouch! That was my ego you just tromped on."

He took her hands and tugged her forward. After dropping a light kiss on her forehead, he drew her into his arms. "That was a compliment, Vassar. And for the record, you're a natural. Hell! You're like exploding dynamite, which is why I almost took you standing up."

Mariah burrowed closer and slid her arms around his waist. As she stood there she sighed softly and basked in the possessive embrace of the tender man who held her, the complex and quite remarkable man who desired her but who also cared enough about her welfare to protect her, the same man who aroused her senses and inspired the love blossoming in her heart.

Jack eventually released her and turned down the light above the drafting table. He and Mariah walked out to the front steps of the verandah.

They sat there for a long time without speaking, holding hands and peering up at the star-studded sky. They listened to the night creatures that roamed the surrounding acreage. Mariah marveled over the simple luxury of sharing a quiet evening with a man she cared for. She felt a sense of contentment that she'd only dreamed about.

"You're a beautiful woman, Mariah Chandler."

She laughed, startled by his comment. "No one's ever accused me of that before, but I'm happy you think so."

"Don't be coy."

"I'm not. My grandmother always told me that beauty was a curse, because men assume a woman is stupid if she's attractive. If a man made the mistake of telling Emma Lacey Chandler that she was beautiful—which she was—then she fired him or scratched him off her guest list."

"I may have to revise my opinion of the lady."

"She wasn't exactly a woman of her time, but she made her independent nature work for her. I admired her. I still do."

Jack withdrew his hand and ran his fingers through his dark hair in a gesture that even sounded frustrated. "I don't understand your marriage to Darren," he said, abruptly changing the subject.

Mariah tensed and her blood chilled at the mention of her ex-husband. His was the last name she wanted to hear, and he was the last person in the world that she wanted to think about at that moment. "Doesn't everyone deserve to make one mistake in judgment?" she asked flippantly.

"Is that what he was? A mistake?"

She got to her feet and made her way down the front steps of the verandah. Turning, she faced Jack. "I don't talk about him. I can't."

"Come back over here and sit down."

"No thanks."

"You freeze up whenever I mention him."

"Do I?"

"And your voice sounds like it's computer-generated."

"Does it?"

Jack muttered a coarse word. "This isn't getting us anywhere. It's too late for you to be walking home alone. Why don't I drop you at the cottage?"

"Fine." Mariah took the few steps to the passenger door of the truck. Jerking it open before Jack could stop her, she climbed in. He caught the door before she closed it and leaned down. Mariah turned away, and his kiss connected with her cheek. She didn't even flinch when he slammed the door and strode around to the driver's side.

Mariah said nothing as Jack drove to the cottage. She felt cold inside, all the warmth generated by their intimacy at the mansion a distant memory. Jack's preoccupation with Darren bothered her. Although she needed to understand the cause of his curiosity and knew she couldn't avoid the subject of her ex-husband forever, a part of her resented the necessity of even mentioning his name.

She left the truck without assistance the instant Jack pulled into the driveway behind her Mercedes. He left the motor running and followed her to the front steps of the cottage.

Mariah paused in the doorway after unlocking the door, the light shining down on her face revealing her strained features.

"He betrayed people," Jack said. "That was his speciality."

"You aren't telling me anything I don't already know about him."

"How could you marry him?"

"I said I don't talk about him, Jack," she reminded him once more as she reached for the inside light switch.

Jack's gaze slid past her and settled on the iron-frame bed. Had he not mentioned Darren, she would have wanted to share that bed with him—tonight and every night. She loved him, but she felt almost relieved, she realized, that they couldn't be intimate yet, because there were truths she needed to reveal before they made love. Truths that would be painful, but truths she couldn't ignore any longer. Otherwise, Darren would, for all practical purposes, be there in bed with them like an evil specter.

Jack placed his hands on her shoulders before she could slip inside. She met his gaze. "It's late, and I need to be up early in the morning."

"We have to talk, Mariah."

She nodded. "I know, but not now."

"It's up to you, but you can't avoid the truth forever."

"I realize that," she conceded.

He studied her, his expression intent. "You aren't the empty-headed, self-serving creature I wanted you to be."

"Am I supposed to apologize?" she asked. "Why in the world would you feel the need to categorize me that way? I know you aren't generally sexist, but what did you expect to accomplish by trying to diminish my value as a person?"

Looking very uncomfortable, he shrugged. "I'm not sure."

"You owe me an explanation, Jack."

"That makes us even, doesn't it?"

"Yes," she whispered. "And you'll have one."

"Great. I can't wait." He turned and walked back to his truck.

Mariah whispered, "Great, but I *can* wait." Reluctantly closing the door, she secured the lock, stepped out of her shoes, and sank down onto the love seat. Despite her fatigue, she hardly slept at all that night.

SEVEN

Jack stood at the edge of the high-ceilinged ball-room, which was rapidly filling with affluent supporters of the Chandler Foundation fund-raiser. Attired in a black tuxedo and crisp white dress shirt, he looked darkly sensual and somewhat mysterious.

Several women studied him with hungry expressions on their faces. Four of them even paused in front of him and attempted to draw his interest, but he just nodded politely and then ignored them. Neither did he feel compelled to join any of the growing clusters of chatting people who sipped champagne and sampled hors d'oeuvres from trays circulated by a legion of waiters.

Jack cupped a snifter of cognac in the palm of his hand, his attention completely focused on

Mariah. Unaware of his decision to attend the charity art auction, she hadn't noticed him yet, and that was the way he wanted it for now. He felt the need to observe this side of Mariah Chandler, the public side that she rarely mentioned, the side that he now suspected extended far beyond a simple figurehead position with a nationally respected charitable organization.

Mariah stood in the receiving line at the entrance to the main ballroom of the Montecito Country Club, flanked by local dignitaries, an array of celebrities, and several notables from the Santa Barbara social scene. He watched her greet each guest with a handshake and a warm smile. She appeared at ease, and Jack quickly concluded that she'd had plenty of experience being in a receiving line on behalf of the Chandler Foundation.

He noticed, with no small amount of amazement, that the women moving through the receiving line seemed unthreatened by her style and beauty, despite the fact that their male escorts paused to chat with Mariah. Unlike Delia, who always managed to alienate every woman with her need to be at the center of attention at any social gathering, Mariah treated everyone she spoke to with equal graciousness.

Clad in a low-cut, floor-length, black silk evening gown that sheathed her body like a second skin and had probably been designed just for her, she appeared sophisticated and self-confident. Absent was the woman who dressed casually at the job site, chewed off her lipstick before she finished her first cup of coffee each morning, ate a sack lunch with a group of construction workers as though it were something she did every day, and wore her hair in an untidy braid down her back. This woman, expertly coiffed, elegantly attired, and artfully made up, would have felt at home at the White House. Jack started to wonder just how many times she'd visited the place.

He experienced an unexpected surge of pride as he continued to study Mariah. She clearly felt comfortable in her role as director of the Chandler Foundation and in dealing with illustrious people.

The guest list included many industrial, creative, and entrepreneurial leaders of California. Jack personally knew several, and could identify the rest by name. A few were even aware of his personal history, because they were also transplanted Virginians, but they respected his privacy and never questioned the choices he'd made ten years earlier.

Like most of the men and women present, Jack preferred anonymity when it came to his personal wealth. His name rarely appeared on mailing lists for charities. He selected the ones he felt inclined to support, and he did so on his own terms. In return, the recipients of his generosity respected his privacy.

It took nearly an hour, but Mariah finally excused herself from the receiving line. Jack watched her make her way down a long hallway that paralleled the ballroom and led to a small patio overlooking the club's golf course. He handed his empty brandy snifter to a passing waiter and followed her. Familiar with the layout of the country club as a longtime member, he took an alternate route to the same location. He stepped into view as she walked out onto the patio. Jack knew by her sudden smile that his decision to follow her had been a good one.

"Taking a break?" he asked as he took her arm and guided her in the direction of a sheltered area at the end of the patio.

"How did you guess?"

"You have that look on your face."

She laughed. "The look that says my shoes are new and my feet hurt?"

He released her and lounged against the wrought-iron railing that circled the patio. "The look that says you need to play hooky for a little while. You've got a good turnout."

"It's wonderful, isn't it?" She searched his features, then asked, "Why didn't you tell me you were going to be here?"

He shrugged. "I show up at worthwhile functions every now and again."

"I'm glad you consider the Chandler Foundation worthwhile."

"It seems important to you."

"Is that why you're here?"

He nodded. "Partly."

"Thank you for caring."

"I care, Vassar," Jack said quietly, realizing that he did indeed care about what her commitment to the foundation said about her as a person.

She glanced away, emotion filling her eyes. He followed her gaze to the sprawling golf course, his curiosity roused as she fought for control. He couldn't remember seeing her with her emotions this close to the surface.

He reached out and caught one of her hands. Lacing their fingers together, he asked, "Are you feeling all right?"

She blinked and focused on him, her smile absent now. "I'm fine. Just a little tired and a lot sad about the way we parted the other night."

"We need to talk."

Mariah nodded. "I'm willing, Jack, whenever you're ready."

"Soon."

A waiter approached them. Mariah took a champagne goblet from the tray he held. Once the young man departed, she took a sip and remarked, "You look very handsome tonight."

Jack tugged her between his legs. His gaze dipped to the swell of her breasts. His body hardened as his eyes lingered on the cleavage that was revealed by the deep V neckline of her gown. "You look too good. That dress reminds me of a pair of gloves I used to own. The fit was excellent."

Mariah smiled. "I take it you approve."

"Most definitely."

"I'm glad."

His voice dropped to an intimate drawl. "Did you dress with me in mind?"

"How could I? I didn't know you'd be here."

"That's not what I asked you."

"I thought of you while I was getting dressed," Mariah admitted. "Satisfied?"

"Thank you. I'm not satisfied, but I intend for us both to be very satisfied at some point in the not-too-distant future."

She blinked in surprise, but she avoided the latter part of his comments. "I didn't do anything worthy of a thank-you."

"Yes, you did, and you know it."

"I really didn't know you'd be attending tonight. You must be on the top-secret guest list. I've discovered that almost every local foundation manager has one."

Jack shrugged, but he didn't admit that he'd agreed almost two months earlier to participate in the fund-raiser by donating two paintings that he intended to reclaim during the art auction. "I received an invitation, so I'm here."

She studied him for a long moment. "Nothing you do is that simple."

He couldn't help grinning at her puzzled expression. "I've surprised you."

"Not really," she insisted.

"Then why do you look confused?"

"You're very good at concealing your thoughts and emotions. I never quite know what you're thinking."

"Would you like to know what I'm thinking right now?"

Mariah's skepticism showed. "Is that a trick question?"

He tugged her closer. The intimate alignment of their bodies made her hand shake. Leaning against Jack, she placed her champagne goblet on a small table near the railing. His body responded instantly to the press of her plump breasts and the fragrance of her skin. Mariah straightened to meet his gaze, but she didn't pull away. Still propped against the railing, he bracketed her hips between his muscular thighs. Their loins were not quite touching, but close enough to fire his blood and his imagination.

She held her breath. Jack felt the delicate shudder that moved through her slender body. The hunger that had become a constant gnawing sensation deep inside him escalated to a muscle-knotting tension that tightened his entire body. He regretted the absence of complete privacy, because he longed for the satisfaction he knew he would find in her arms.

Mariah slid her hands beneath his unbuttoned jacket. Pressing her palms against the hard wall of his chest, she kneaded the muscles beneath her fingertips, her breath moving quickly in and out of her body, her eyes darkening to midnight-blue pools as her head tilted to one side.

Jack clamped down on his desire, which threatened to send him spinning out of control. His voice rough, he said, "I'm thinking that we should be alone right now, Vassar. I'm thinking about how much I'd like to peel that length of silk off your body one inch at a time. I want to explore every bit of you with my mouth and hands."

"Jack . . ." she whispered, her cheeks flushed.

He circled her narrow waist with his hands and urged her closer still. Despite the torture of not being able to take her then and there, he positioned her so that her pelvis pressed against the pulsing strength of his maleness. She shimmied against him, eyes wide and riveted on his face.

The fabric that separated their bodies did nothing to stop the currents of desire flowing between them. Jack possessed neither the strength nor the will to pull back. Instead, they tantalized each other with an implicit promise of intimacy.

"I want to kiss you all over until you're breathless, Mariah, and I want to make love to you until neither one of us can string enough words together to make a coherent sentence. And then I want to start at the beginning and do it all over again. Now you know exactly what I'm thinking."

He felt utterly seduced by her as she stared at him, a startled look in her eyes and the tip of her tongue skimming along the seam of her lips as she nervously moistened them.

"I could eat you alive," he breathed.

Her hands slid higher beneath his jacket. They curved over his broad shoulders a moment before she gripped him for balance. Jack shuddered.

Mariah whispered his name. He bent his head and dropped a kiss onto her exposed shoulder. He felt intoxicated by the softness and scent of her skin. She shivered as his lips swept across her shoulder, then sighed a moment later, the sound an inarticulate invitation that Jack didn't ignore. He teased her with hot kisses as he traced a line up her neck with his lips. Pausing at her diamond-studded earlobe, he flicked his tongue against it, then gently teethed the tender flesh.

Mariah clung to him and trembled in his arms. Jack felt the storm moving through her. Straightening, he gathered her into a tighter embrace. She looped her arms around his neck, blindly seeking comfort and closeness. Her lips brushed over the sensitive skin beneath his chin. She nuzzled his throat like an affectionate cat, and as he held her and breathed deeply of her unique fragrance, he felt the frantic patter of her heart.

"Nothing to say, Vassar?" he finally managed to ask.

She lifted her head to peer up at him. "I don't know where to begin."

"Are you sure?"

She moaned in obvious frustration, the sound faint but incredibly seductive.

"I know where to start."

She eased backward. Despite his reluctance to allow her to separate their upper bodies, he didn't try to stop her. She remained standing between his legs, the intimate alignment undisturbed.

Mariah sighed heavily. "I think it's going to be a very long evening."

"You sound out of breath," he teased as he smoothed his hands up and down her slender arms. He couldn't not touch her, he realized. She was an invitation he couldn't resist.

"Do I?"

He nodded. "Shall we end it together?"

She gave him a bemused look. "End what?"

"The evening."

"I'd be disappointed if we didn't."

"Why?" he asked, his low voice barely audible.

"Because I want you," she said. "I want you so much that I'm on the verge of forgetting why I'm here tonight."

He thrust his hips forward as he pressed his fingers against the base of her spine. The evidence of his arousal expressed his need, and he felt the shiver that rippled through her. "I want you, Mariah Chandler, more than I've ever wanted any woman in my entire life."

Lifting her hand, Mariah traced the width of his lower lip with a fingertip. "I love your mouth. I want a taste of you, Jack."

"You're playing with fire," he cautioned.

"I think I knew that." Mariah paused, her fingertip lingering near the edge of his lips. "Do you mind?"

"Hardly." He studied her features, the dreamy expression on her face revealing many of her thoughts, but he discovered that he wanted to know more. "What are you thinking right now?"

"I didn't know I could feel this way."

"Tell me how you feel," he urged.

Mariah withdrew her hand. Jack caught it, brought her fingertips to his lips, and pressed a kiss to the tip of each one. A flash of surprise widened her eyes. He'd seen it before, and he suddenly wondered why any overt display of tenderness seemed like a new experience for her.

"Do you promise not to laugh at me?" she asked almost shyly.

He nodded. The impulse to protect and cherish expanded inside him. Startled, Jack questioned the wisdom of allowing himself to even feel such entangling emotions.

Mariah exhaled shakily before she spoke. "I feel like a piece of ripe fruit that needs to be picked."

"And eaten," he finished for her, his senses aflame once again.

"And eaten," she echoed, her voice a sensual little whisper.

Jack closed his eyes as he gathered her back into his arms. A shudder ripped through him. Another one quickly followed. When he finally found a remnant of the self-control he'd always prized in himself, he focused on Mariah's face. He glimpsed a hunger in her gaze that was more honest than anything he'd ever seen in his entire life.

He glanced beyond her to assure himself that they hadn't drawn an audience. After trailing his fingers up the length of her spine, he smoothed the tips across her nape. She shivered, twisting sensuously against his hard body. Cupping her face with his hands, he leaned down.

He took her lips, feeling them tremble and then part. Her tongue darted forward to meet his, tentatively at first, then more boldly. Jack sensed that she was testing herself, breaking new ground. It still puzzled him, this lack of experience. He needed to understand it. He needed to understand Mariah Chandler. Jack silently vowed that he would just as she mounted a new assault on his senses. He succumbed to the sweet sensations Mariah evoked as she nibbled at his lower lip, her tender aggression unleashing a molten flow of glittering sensation into his bloodstream.

She whimpered into his mouth as he wrapped his arms more securely around her. The sound of her need tore through him. Angling his head, he deepened their kiss even more, too hungry for her to be cautious, too needy at that moment to care about the possibility of prying eyes. She tasted of champagne and passion, a heady mix of flavors that aroused his body to the point of physical pain. He sampled her like a connoisseur. She responded, expressing her desire without restraint.

Jack groaned when he felt her fingertips glide down to his muscled belly. Her brief hesitation when she reached his cummerbund allowed him a moment of rationality. Reluctantly brushing aside her hands, he realized that he wanted her intimate touch almost as much as he wanted air to breathe, but this wasn't the place.

Freeing her lips, Jack gripped her shoulders and gently nudged her backward. He bowed his head, his respiration choppy, his heart racing. The feel of her palms pressed against his cheeks a few moments later prompted him to lift his head and meet her gaze. He exhaled, the heavy gust of air a sign of his shaky control.

"You're hell on my good intentions, Vassar. I was trying to be a gentleman tonight."

Mariah smiled, her expression almost whimsical. Her fingers shook as she stroked them through his thick dark hair. "You're you, Jack. You're all I want."

"I doubt that."

As he fought for control he thought for a moment about the tension that had existed between them during those first weeks at the mansion. Unanswered questions still hovered between them, regardless of their truce, regardless of the desire that raged between them like an out-of-control brushfire every time they got near each other.

She studied his expression as she lowered her hands to her sides, the tenderness in her gaze remaining even though her smile faded. "Your mind's going a hundred miles a second, isn't it? You're thinking about all the things we still need to talk about."

Jack didn't bother to deny the obvious.

"I don't know how you manage to think at a time like this." She absently smoothed a wrinkle from the front of her gown as she looked past him. "I feel so out of control when this happens between us." Mariah looked at him. "It's a new feeling, but I like it."

Need still suffusing every cell in his body, Jack held her face between his callused hands. "Don't feel alone, Mariah. This is different, and I'm glad." He heard footsteps and glanced at the entrance to the patio. "Vivian Witherspoon's headed our way." The alarm in Mariah's eyes made him realize that she felt more than a little vulnerable. "Take a deep breath. Vivian's not the judgmental type."

Although she looked unnerved, Mariah composed herself before turning to greet Vivian Witherspoon.

She was a good-natured soul in her midthirties with six children and an assortment of dogs and cats that had her husband lamenting the fact that they were always on the edge of bankruptcy thanks to the grocery bills. "Shame on you, Jack," she teased. "You aren't supposed to kidnap the guest of honor at a fund-raiser."

Jack grinned as he embraced her. He then stepped back to stand beside Mariah. "It's good to see you, Viv. How're the kids?"

"They're fine, Jack. No broken arms this week, the cats haven't been shaved by my younger two, and I've had to replace only one retainer since Monday, but there's no telling what I'll discover when I get home tonight."

He chuckled.

"I'm delighted you decided to join us. The paintings . . ."

He gave her a cautioning look, his message obvious to Vivian, who knew him quite well.

" . . . the paintings are just beautiful," she said, accepting his cue without missing a beat or drawing Mariah's curiosity. "Have you toured our makeshift gallery yet?"

"When I arrived."

Mariah commented, "Everyone's been very generous."

Vivian smiled. "This is a very generous community. People don't always realize it, though. We're all ready for you, my dear."

Glancing at Jack, Mariah clarified the situation. "Time for me to get to work."

He took her hand and squeezed her fingers. He heard the shallow breath that escaped her as she returned the squeeze.

"I'll look for you later, all right?"

"I'll be here," he promised, his gaze hot and possessive.

Mariah smiled, her eyes filled with an emotion that reminded Jack of relief. He suddenly realized that she still felt uncertain about him. When, he asked himself as he watched the two women walk away, had he allowed her to feel the least bit secure? He'd deliberately kept her off balance, but now he questioned the need. Only her resilience had held her steadfast in the face of his adversarial behavior.

Filled with admiration for Mariah's strength and innocence, Jack followed the two women at a leisurely pace as they made their way back to the crowded ballroom. He chuckled when he heard Vivian casually say, "I didn't realize you and Jack were such good friends."

Though Mariah replied, "We're working together on a very special project," Jack knew that Vivian had already figured out that something was up between them. Fortunately, she wasn't a gossip. Still, he appreciated Mariah's understated response. He approved of her apparent reluctance to shout the intimate details of her life from the rooftops.

Jack lingered on the periphery of the ball-room while Mariah and Vivian made their way to the podium on the far side of the room. He kept Mariah in view, a task easily accomplished thanks to his height.

Mariah paused several times before she reached the podium, her poise and easy smile once again drawing people to her like a magnet. She never charmed with deliberation, he realized, only with genuine warmth. Delia, on the other hand, calculated the impact of every word, every action like a choreographer staging dance steps. He knew now that Delia had been motivated by greed and a constant craving for adulation from all quarters.

"Ladies and gentlemen, may I have your attention, please?" Vivian Witherspoon smiled at the crowd as they quieted. "Good evening, and welcome to the annual Chandler Founda-tion fund-raiser. As most of you already know, our guest of honor this evening is the national director of the Chandler Foundation. Mariah has served in that capacity for the last five years. She dislikes lengthy introductions, especially the ones that extol her virtues as national director. She prefers not to have your recognition of her lead-ership, insight, and sensitivity to the problems faced by battered women and their children. She hopes, instead, that your attention will remain on their needs as you participate in this fund-raiser. I take great pride in calling this woman of compassion and kindness my friend. Please join me now in welcoming the director of the Chandler Foundation, Mariah Lacey Chandler."

The applause that followed was enthusiastic, not simply polite.

Mariah stepped up to the microphone. "Thank you all for joining us this evening. You realize, I'm certain, that we're expecting a lot from you when you reach for your checkbooks this evening. I want to assure you that the funds you donate will all go to local foundation-sponsored shelters for victims of spousal abuse and their children. The day-to-day operations of the Chandler Foundation are funded separately from a trust account established more than thirty years ago by my late grandmother, Emma Lacey Chandler. She believed that all donated monies should go directly to the intended recipients, and I'm pleased to tell you that that tradition continues."

Jack couldn't keep his eyes off her as she spoke. Despite the distance between them, she looked at him the entire time. He sensed that she needed him to understand what motivated her. Unaware of anyone but Mariah as he listened to her, he absorbed the intensity and commitment that blazed like a beacon of light within her.

He'd seen her this way before. When she'd been in his arms, caught up in the passion that flowed like a combustible fluid between them, and when she'd fought so tenaciously to make a space for herself in the restoration process at the mansion.

Clearly the driving force behind the success of the foundation, Mariah had a strength of character that he'd resisted acknowledging during the past few months, a strength and grace he couldn't ignore or deny any longer.

His conclusions about Mariah had been skewed by a lingering bitterness connected to his past. He wondered if once he understood her marriage to Darren, he could let go of the fear of betrayal that had haunted him for so many years, not just his anxiety that if he allowed himself to be happy, his life wouldn't collapse around him like a house of cards.

" . . . in my five years as the director of the foundation, the generosity of people like you has allowed us to open more than three dozen shelters across the country. Our research staff, along with field personnel dispatched from our headquarters in Washington and local foundation managers, aid us in targeting communities with the greatest need. As the stresses of daily life escalate, so do the incidents of family violence. I believe that we have an obligation as a society to rescue the victims of this violence. With your assistance, the Chandler Foundation is dedicated to providing secure environments for victims of spousal abuse as they receive counseling, assistance in caring for their children, job training, and attorney guidance as they navigate the waters of the legal system. We are also working with our local and national legislators in an effort to promote laws that will protect the rights of abused spouses."

Mariah paused and looked around the room. "My hope this evening is that you will express your support of our efforts with generosity, as you have so many times in the past." She smiled. "Thank you for caring enough to join us tonight, and thank you for sharing in our commitment to improve the lives of those we serve through the Chandler Foundation."

Applause exploded, enthusiastic applause that didn't wane as Vivian replaced Mariah at the podium. Vivian waited several minutes. She then outlined the rules for the auction as a partition behind her was swept aside to reveal the makeshift gallery of paintings, sculptures, and other objets d'art. Dinner and dancing, she announced, would follow the auction.

Jack half listened to Vivian's comments as he watched Mariah disappear into the crowd that clustered around her the instant she stepped off the stage. As he exited the ballroom in search of a few minutes of privacy, he realized that he had to rethink all of his assumptions about Mariah Chandler. If he didn't, he sensed that he would lose her. And he knew in his heart that he couldn't risk that kind of a loss.

EIGHT

After nearly two hours of circulating among the guests, Mariah spotted Jack as the auction came to a close. He'd participated in the auction and was now handing Vivian his personal check. She stood close enough to hear their conversation.

"When would you like me to pick them up?" he asked as he tucked his wallet into the breast pocket of his tuxedo jacket.

"The paintings will be recrated and available tomorrow afternoon. Thank you again, Jack." Vivian glanced at the check. "This will be the single largest donation of the fund-raiser. You still don't want it mentioned in our press release?"

"That was our agreement," Jack reminded her.

"And we'll honor it. I'm sure you'll be glad to have the paintings back in your collection."

He smiled. "I have grown rather attached to them over the years."

"Who wouldn't?" Vivian exclaimed. "They're remarkable."

Jack smiled. "Tell Bill and the kids hello for me." As he turned to leave he spotted Mariah.

She approached him, happy that they'd finally found each other in the crush of guests. Her smile concealed her surprise over the two paintings and his substantial donation.

"I'm impressed, Mariah Chandler," he told her as he linked their hands.

Respecting his desire for privacy regarding his contribution to the foundation, she said, "The paintings you selected are beautiful. I would have bid on them myself if I hadn't stopped to chat with the Conrads."

"I wasn't talking about the paintings."

"What, then?" she asked.

He led her out of the gallery area and into the less populated hallway. "You, Vassar. I'm very impressed with you."

Mariah moved closer, delight resonating within her that he seemed to comprehend and appreciate her involvement in the Chandler Foundation. "That's a two-way street, you know. Besides, I was just doing my job."

Jack slipped his arm around her waist as they found a quiet alcove and stood in front of a window that overlooked a small courtyard. A soft rain had begun to fall, blurring their reflections.

"Your *job* is a hell of a lot more important than counting paper clips."

"You're right, but I do that, too, when I'm trying to figure out how I'm going to inspire people at fund-raisers."

"Right."

"Don't be so cynical," she chided with a laugh. "I'm serious. I struggle with speeches, probably because I have such a profound aversion to begging for money, no matter how great the need. I finally figured out that I do better if I maintain my dignity and simply share the facts and my own feelings when I'm trying to persuade people to see the merit of contributing to the foundation. It works most of the time."

"You had them eating out of your hand."

"I doubt that, but I do think I conveyed my conviction that the foundation serves a worthy purpose." She turned in the half circle of his encompassing arm. "You sound very much the same when you talk about your work. It's simple, actually. It's called commitment."

He rubbed his chin, his expression speculative. "You've been organizing this shindig while you've been working at the mansion, haven't you?"

"Grandmother always said that an hour wasted was an hour lost." She shrugged, aware that he'd discovered just how long her days really were. "I keep busy, but I really can't take much credit for the evening's success. I made a few phone calls, that's all. Vivian and her volunteers did the lion's share of the work."

"Why don't I believe you?"

"I wish you would," she said, her gaze riveted to his rugged features. She wanted the evening to end so that they could be alone.

"Mr. McMillan?"

Jack glanced up. Mariah turned, recognizing the voice of the country club's manager.

"Problem, Marty?" he asked.

"Sir, you have an urgent phone call. If you'll follow me, you can use my office."

"I'll wait here," Mariah offered.

"No need."

They walked the short distance to the manager's office. Mariah stood in the doorway while Jack took the call. He said little, mostly listened, but she immediately noticed the tension that stiffened his shoulders and brought a frown to his face.

"I'll be there in fifteen minutes. If he gives you any trouble, tell him I'm on my way," Jack instructed before recradling the receiver and dragging his fingers through his dark hair.

Mariah approached him, concerned. "What's wrong?"

He glanced at her. "Tommy's managed to wrap his car around a telephone pole. He doesn't have any family in the area. The hospital knows he works for me, so they decided to track me down."

"Is he . . ." Mariah didn't want to ask the question, but she did anyway. "It's serious, isn't it?"

"He's pretty banged up, but he'll be all right. The nurses are having a problem with him, though. He's got that macho act of his perfected to a science, and the fact that he has a mild concussion and a compound fracture of his right leg doesn't seem to be getting his attention. The doctor's threatening to use restraints on him if he doesn't settle down and cooperate."

"Would you like some company? I might be able to help."

Jack shook his head. "Five hundred people might decide to lynch me if you disappear on them now. Besides, I shouldn't be gone long. I'll try to make it back in time for dessert."

"I'll walk out with you."

"I'm not quite ready to leave," he said as he took a seat on the edge of the manager's desk and drew her into a loose embrace.

"I don't want you to leave," she said softly. Circling his neck with her hands, she drew his head down and kissed him. A kiss of invitation. A kiss filled with promises. A kiss that reflected her desire for him. A kiss that reminded her of her grandmother's comment about being willing to risk everything for the right man.

Jack McMillan was the right man. He was, she realized as she stroked his cheek with her fingertips, the man she loved. His gaze, so hot and covetous as he looked at her from beneath partially lowered lashes, made her feel like the only woman in the world. "I'll miss you," she whispered.

He groaned. "What you do to me has to be illegal."

She grinned at him. "Do you want me to check the local statutes?"

His scorching gaze settled on her breasts, making her nipples harden.

"Just hold my place, Vassar. We're going to finish what we keep starting."

"I want you, Jack."

"And I want you," he muttered before he dropped a kiss on her lips. "Tommy has the worst timing. I'm tempted to dock him a week's pay for this little stunt."

He left her then, left her with an expression of genuine regret etched into his features, the musky scent of his cologne invading her senses, the memory of that seductive half smile of his that made her bones feel like hot candle wax, and the knowledge that their time was close at hand.

The meal served by the country club was excellent. At least that was what everyone at the table told her, but Mariah didn't notice. She sampled the food on her plate out of courtesy to the chef, and she responded politely when spoken to by her tablemates. For the most part, though, she listened to the rain, unseasonable for this time of year, as it splattered the floor-to-ceiling windows near her table.

The weather continued to worsen, the rain becoming a heavy downpour. Lightning, an equally uncommon event for coastal California, slashed through the night sky at unexpected moments.

Mariah lingered until the last guest departed, hopeful that Jack would make his way back to the country club. She worried that Tommy had developed complications, but she didn't know which hospital to call for information. She worried that Jack might have had an accident on the narrow, rain-slick back roads that connected Santa Barbara and Montecito.

Fatigue and disappointment, she chastised herself, were making her imagine the worst possible scenarios. Mariah finally gave up on Jack when all the chairs and tables had been cleared out of the ballroom by the housekeeping staff.

She claimed her car, and as she buckled her seat belt she decided that Jack had to have an excellent reason for not returning to the country club, although she wondered what it was.

The limited visibility made her cautious as she slowly drove through the hills of Santa Barbara. When her car suddenly died, Mariah guided it to the edge of the road. She tried the ignition several times, but without success. She waited for nearly fifteen minutes, hoping that a Good Samaritan would come by and notice her blinking emergency lights. Much to her dismay, no one did. There was nothing else to do but walk to the nearest residence and call for a tow truck.

Mariah moved with care in the dark, her hair, long silk gown, and shoes saturated within seconds. Thunder boomed overhead. The trees on either side of the road trembled violently in the wind, the sound eerie.

She nearly jumped out of her skin when she heard a car horn blare a few minutes later. Mariah glanced over her shoulder and was relieved when she recognized Jack as the driver of the car that pulled up beside her.

"Get in!" he shouted above the gusting wind.

"I'm soaking wet."

"Do you think I care?" he demanded as he leaned over to open the door.

Mariah settled into the leather passenger seat. Jack shrugged out of his jacket and draped it over her shoulders.

"Are you all right? What happened?" he asked.

"I'm fine, just wet and cold. The engine stopped, but I don't know why. When I couldn't get it to start again, I thought I'd better look for a phone."

Jack flipped a switch on the dashboard and hot air blasted into the car. "You need a hot shower and dry clothes."

After calling a towing service from his car phone, Jack drove off. He took a route she didn't recognize, but she quickly realized why when instead of arriving at the mansion, he guided his car up a long, unfamiliar driveway. He activated a garage-door opener and pulled into a triple-wide garage.

"It's another fifteen minutes to your place," he said as he shoved open the car door.

Mariah followed Jack into the house, her teeth chattering from the chill moving through her body. She quickly registered the sweeping lines and vaulted ceilings of the house as he led her down a long hallway to what appeared to be a guest bathroom. He turned on the shower, then handed her a stack of towels and urged, "Get in there and warm up while I find you something to wear."

After Jack closed the bathroom door, Mariah undressed. She stepped into the shower, savoring the warmth of the water as she unpinned her hair and shook it loose. When she was done, she found what looked like the top of a pair of men's pajamas on the counter by the sink. The top reached down to the middle of her thighs, the scent clinging to the material reminding her of Jack the moment she slipped it over her head. After rolling up the sleeves, she searched her purse for a comb and ran it through her wet hair, which she left loose to dry naturally.

Mariah heard the sound of another shower running when she opened the bathroom door and walked into the hallway. She wandered through the house, admiring its sleek contemporary lines, the thick beige Berber area rugs, and the burgundy leather furniture that dominated the living room.

Her wandering led her to what she decided must be Jack's study. A spacious room with floor-to-ceiling windows along one entire wall, the study contained an oak desk, a matching drafting table, several comfortable chairs, and well-placed lights that suggested that Jack did a great deal of his work at home.

Framed certificates and plaques adorned one wall, and bookshelves overflowed with literary offerings. She paused near a collection of architectural models enclosed in glass and situated atop pedestals. She recognized them as models for buildings that had won top design awards in the architectural world.

Why, she wondered, had Jackson McMillan Wainright III traded one identity for another? Why was he living what amounted to a lie?

Jack found her in his office. She stood with her back to him as she studied one particular high-rise model that he'd designed at the start of his career. With her hair tumbling down her back, her long legs exposed to his view, and his shirt dwarfing her slender figure, she epitomized a classic blend of sensuality and innocence.

He gave little attention to the object of her interest as he paused in the doorway, his gaze sweeping over her, his loins throbbing with long-suppressed desire beneath the jeans he wore. Moving silently into the room on bare feet, Jack placed his hands on her shoulders and turned her around so that they faced each other.

With a smile on her face, she slid her arms around his waist and pressed her cheek against his muscled chest. Nuzzling the springy dark hair that triangled down the front of his torso, she inhaled the musky scent of man and soap and savored the warmth radiating from his skin. His heartbeat thudded beneath her ear, the pace escalating as she molded her body to his.

"Feel better?" he asked as he ran his hands up and down her back.

Mariah looked up. "Much better. Warm too. Thank you."

"For what?"

"For riding to my rescue."

"My pleasure."

"Tommy? Is he all right?"

Jack nodded. "A little scared, even though he had trouble admitting it for a while. I called his folks in San Diego. They're coming up tomorrow."

He slipped his arm around her shoulders, guiding her out of the study and into the living room. A fire blazed in the fireplace. They sank down onto a pile of cushions in front of it. Two partially filled brandy snifters sat on the edge of the hearth. Jack helped himself after handing one to Mariah.

Without thinking of the potential consequences, she voiced her earlier curiosity. "Why did you leave everything behind, Jack? Why did you just walk away? You gave up so much, and it doesn't make any sense."

He froze, shock in his dark eyes. Mariah returned her snifter to the edge of the hearth and took his hand before he could get to his feet and walk away. She didn't let go, even though he closed it into a fist between her palms.

"Don't pull away from me, please."

"Then don't pry into my past. It doesn't concern you."

"Why are you living a lie?" she asked, her grip on him tightening.

Jack glared at her, the implacable expression on his face and his silence conveying his unwillingness to speak about the life and the marriage he'd abandoned ten years earlier.

Mariah sighed in frustration, but she forged ahead. "If you won't talk to me about your past, then I guess I'll have to tell you about mine. I suspect it's the only way you'll ever trust me enough to open up, and I've put this conversation off for too long as it is."

"I don't want to hear it."

She released his fist and pressed her palms together. Gathering her inner strength, she stared into the flames that danced above the logs in the fireplace. "Of course you do. You've asked me about Darren several times, and I think this is a good time to give you an answer."

"I'm not interested in anything except getting you into my bed. The rest can wait."

As if to prove his point, Jack set aside his brandy, took her by the waist, and turned her so that she faced him. He tumbled her back against the cushions and came down over her, his hips lodging between her parted thighs, his arms bracing his weight above her. He slowly settled against her, the heat of his body easing into hers like a molten flow.

Mariah shuddered when his hands closed over her breasts, then she arched into his touch. Jack took her lips, his hunger making him almost ruthless as he plundered her mouth and caressed her breasts with clever fingers. Her nipples instantly tightened into hard buds, the tunic covering them a barrier that he quickly stripped from her body.

He cupped her breasts, drawing a gasp from her with the possessive nature of his touch. "I don't want to talk, Mariah. In fact, talking's the last thing on my mind." He leaned down, drawing one of her nipples into his mouth.

She strained up from the cushions, her fingers plunging into his thick dark hair. She held his head as he suckled her, moaning low in her throat. Every nerve in her body came alive with sensations even as a single tear slid down her cheek. Another followed. Then another, until they blended and formed narrow streams down her cheeks.

Jack lifted his head, shock etching his features when he saw the wet tracks on Mariah's face. She wept for him, but not because of anything he'd done. She wept because she felt the darkness that shadowed his heart and kept him from expressing his emotions.

Jack lowered his forehead to the valley between her breasts, his breathing choppy. "Mariah . . . say whatever it is that you need to say. I'll listen."

She nodded as he freed her, but she didn't meet his gaze. She wiped her cheeks with the backs of her hands, and this time when she reached for his hands, he didn't resist. If anything, Mariah sensed that he needed her touch as much as she did his at that moment.

Drawing in a steadying breath, she said quietly, "I've had a rule since my marriage ended. I never discuss Darren with anyone."

Jack gave her a troubled look. "Maybe we should keep it that way."

"We can't. He's an invisible but very real barrier between us that needs to be destroyed once and for all. Other than my grandmother and a therapist I saw for nearly two years after our marriage ended, I've never spoken to anyone about him. I'm going to break my rule tonight for a couple of reasons. I can't make love to you if we don't talk about him, and you need to stop being so defensive with me."

She studied his wary expression. Despite her openness, she felt anxious about his reaction to what she intended to tell him. "I want us to be together, but the right way and for the right reasons. I don't want secrets between us. I understand pain and the anger that comes with it, Jack, and I can feel yours when the past is mentioned, but if you can't find a way to stop using your suspicion as a shield to protect your feelings, then we'll never be anything more than two people who happened to crawl between the sheets for a one-night stand. I want more than that, and I think you do too."

He exhaled harshly. "I don't think of you as a one-night stand."

"You won't want to, but that's what I'll become. I may be less experienced than most women of thirty-two, but I'm not stupid. You've been suspicious of me and my motives for wanting you to handle the restoration since our first moments together. At first, I thought you were just being temperamental, but then I came to the conclusion that my marriage to Darren was the reason for your hostile attitude. I swear to you on everything I hold dear that he hasn't been a part of my life, other than in the form of a bad memory, since the day I left him, and he has absolutely nothing to do with the restoration of Chandler House, although I'm certain now that you once believed he did."

Jack looked uncomfortable, but he nodded in agreement. The truth, he realized, was in her face. Darren *was* a part of Mariah's past. For whatever reason, their marriage ended. They weren't in league together to destroy everything he'd worked for during the last ten years, although he'd believed that until recently. Mariah wasn't capable of the kind of duplicity that Delia had practiced, and he felt like a fool for thinking she could have been.

"When I married your stepbrother, I was young, innocent until my wedding night, and so naive about relationships between men and women that I didn't recognize his moral bankruptcy for what it was. He swept me off my feet. I didn't see his attention and his declarations of love for what they were. An elaborate ploy, and nothing more. It took me a while, but I finally discovered his real interests in life. Money, gambling, and other women. When he didn't get what he wanted, he hurt people, deliberately and with incredible cruelty."

Jack frowned. He tilted his head to one side, studying her for a long moment before he asked, "What exactly are you saying?"

"I'm saying that he abused me emotionally, and when that didn't work, he used his fists on me. He started small, smacking me in places where the bruises wouldn't show, but then he got careless. It's hard finding excuses for constant black eyes, sprained wrists, and broken ribs, so I went out less and less. He nearly destroyed my self-esteem and self-confidence; he demeaned me at every opportunity, even in front of friends, and he put me in the hospital on more than a half-dozen occasions during our last two years together." Mariah almost choked on her memories as they came spilling out. Pausing, she took a deep breath and continued, "I'm saying that your stepbrother almost killed me one night when he flew into a rage over the fact that I refused to pay off his gambling debts. I endured that man for five of the longest and loneliest years of my life, and then I left him, with my grandmother's help."

Clearly stunned, Jack struggled for words. "I thought . . . what I thought was obviously wrong," he finally admitted. "He actually used his fists on you?"

Mariah nodded. She saw his horror and disgust, and she remembered when she'd felt those same emotions. Now she simply felt free to live her life.

Opening her hands, he brought each palm to his lips and pressed kisses into them. When he looked at her again, he asked the question she expected, the logical question that her therapist had warned her would be asked.

"Why didn't you leave him the first time he became violent?"

"He'd been drinking, and I told myself that he'd just lost control. I didn't want to believe it would ever happen again, but it did. As time passed I became afraid, humiliated, and I thought that I'd caused his anger. He was very persuasive, especially when he insisted that he loved me and needed me, even though I provoked him into his fits of uncontrollable anger. I was foolish enough to believe him, and stupid enough to think that I could help him change. I was wrong on both counts."

Jack appeared too stunned to say anything more, but Mariah found comfort in the fact that he didn't turn away from her. He tightened his hold on her wrists. His way, she hoped, of conveying his belief that she was speaking the truth and that he was attempting to understand a complex situation that had forced her to start her life over again six years ago.

"Darren is a part of my past, but he's still your stepbrother. Will your relationship with him be a problem for us?" she asked quietly.

"Never." His reply, sharp and quickly stated, startled her, but Mariah recovered quickly.

"He was the only man who ever touched me sexually, but even that was an extension of his cruelty. He was a thoughtless man who couldn't find satisfaction unless he dominated. I didn't like sex when I was married to him. It was a duty, and nothing more," she confessed. "I loathed it after a while, because sex became just one more perverse way for Darren to control me. You . . ." She hesitated, her voice cracking. "You are the only man who has ever touched me as a lover should touch a woman. I meant it when I said I'd had my innocence beaten out of me by an expert. Darren was that expert."

Jack stared at her, expressionless now. Mariah forced herself to go on. "When I first left him, I was afraid of my own shadow. I spent months just sitting in my bedroom at grandmother's and staring at the walls. I didn't have the strength or the will to do anything else. I knew I'd been betrayed, but what I didn't understand then was that I had choices. The counseling I received helped me realize that I could live without fear. It also taught me that men who intimidate women through emotional or physical abuse are cowards.

I know how to defend myself now, and I learned how to turn the emotional paralysis I experienced into something positive. The Chandler Foundation is my outlet. It always will be."

"You've lived the nightmare," Jack said quietly. "And you understand better than most what the victims need in the way of assistance." He extended his arms, respect, not pity, in his gaze. "Come here, Mariah. I need to hold you. I need to feel your warmth, and I need to be sure that you're real and that you're mine."

Blindly, instinctively, Mariah moved forward, accepting the welcome he offered. Relief flowed through her and tears stung her eyes as she surged into his arms. He embraced her, his strength and compassion helping to calm her shaken emotions. While he hadn't said that he loved her, she sensed that Jack accepted her and all the baggage she carried from her past.

Wrapping her arms around his neck, she held on to him tightly. "I believe in love again, and I believe in myself. I trust my own judgments about people now too. I care deeply about you, Jack. I never expected to want a man, but I want you. A sadistic monster who passed himself off as a human being almost destroyed my life, my hope, and my optimism for the future. I won't ever give anyone that kind of power over me again, but I will offer myself to the right man as an equal partner in a loving relationship."

The hands moving soothingly up and down her back slowed to a stop. "Are you offering yourself to me, Mariah?"

"Yes," she whispered. "Oh, yes."

"Is that wise?"

"I told you, I trust myself to make good judgments about people. I know that you'd never deliberately hurt anyone, and I'm absolutely certain that you wouldn't ever hurt me."

"I wouldn't."

She hugged him with every bit of strength she possessed.

"Why were you crying before?" he asked as he continued to stroke her back with gentle hands.

Mariah lifted her cheek from his shoulder and looked at him. "Are you sure you want to know?"

Despite his troubled expression, Jack nodded.

"I think you're afraid to be happy, because it might be snatched away from you when you least expect it."

"That's crazy," he protested.

"Is it?" She reached out and traced the width of his lower lip with her fingertip. "I don't think so." Leaning forward a moment later, she kissed him thoroughly, seductively. "I want us to be lovers, Jack. No one's ever really made love to me. All I've experienced is sex that left me feeling used and heartsick. You've already taught me that there's a difference."

"But we haven't—"

Mariah laughed softly. "My point exactly. We didn't even have to finish what we kept starting," she told him, using his words from earlier that evening. "And I already know that you'll give and not just take." She clasped his face between her two hands. "I want new memories to replace the old ones, unless you have doubts about whether or not you want to take me into your bed and make love to me now that you know the truth about me."

He took one of her hands and pressed it against his maleness, which swelled even more at her touch. "Does that feel like doubt to you?"

Snuggling closer, she kept her hand over him as her breasts plumped against his hard chest. His answering groan and hardening body spoke volumes, as did his powerful embrace.

"I survived hell, Jack, and now I want heaven. Will you give it to me?"

NINE

"I'll give you anything you want," Jack vowed as he surged to his feet. "Anything at all."

She followed him with her eyes. He felt the sweep of her heated gaze, and his body responded. His blood pounded through his veins, as though on a rampage. His senses glittered, and his groin throbbed.

Mariah smiled, the sensual smile of a woman who knows exactly what she wants from her man. Raising her hands, she threaded her fingers through her thick hair. Her breasts swayed gently, the tips puckering with invitation as she lifted her hair off her neck and then slowly released it. It fell in wild disarray across her bare shoulders and down her back.

Jack couldn't quite believe the desire he saw in her face as she smiled at him, but it was there in her beautiful blue eyes and in the glow that flushed her cheeks with color. Gone, he realized, was the melancholy that sharing her past with him had caused. He understood her motive for revealing the truth, and he felt a certain relief that she had. Otherwise . . . He didn't even want to ponder *otherwise*, because he sensed that the wrong move on his part could have permanently ruined sexual intimacy for her. He would have willingly died before subjecting her to such carelessness.

Jack loathed the very idea of the cruelty she'd been forced to endure, just as he loathed the man who'd turned her into his victim, but he felt both pride in Mariah and relief for himself that her spirit had survived and flourished once again. And as much as he hated to admit it, she grasped the anxiety he experienced when his emotions were on the line. But the reasons for his reluctance to speak about his departure from Washington were private and would remain that way. He didn't intend to discuss Delia with anyone. Not even Mariah. Especially not Mariah.

"Anything, Jack?"

"Anything."

"I want you. Only you."

She extended her hands. He reached out to her in the same moment. Drawing her up and into his arms, Jack cradled her against his chest and carried her out of the living room, down the hallway, and into his bedroom.

He pulled back the sheets and the quilt that covered his bed and then lowered her onto the center of it, his dark eyes riveted on her face as he peeled off his jeans and kicked them aside. He came down beside her, his muscled body rigid with desire. Gathering her against him, he felt her eagerness when she shimmied even closer. His manhood surged against her lower abdomen as he embraced the lushness of her figure and inhaled the fragrance of her skin. He knew he could never get enough of her.

"You're sure?" he asked, his voice low and ragged with a kind of need that he'd never before experienced.

She sighed softly, her hands sliding up his chest and across his wide shoulders before her fingers tangled behind his neck. "I've never been more sure of anything in my entire life."

Groaning with disbelief, Jack took her mouth, his tongue plunging into the heat and honey of her passion. He explored her with his hands as he kissed her, eagerly tracing the curves and hollows of her naked body with skilled, knowing fingers. He savored her trembling response and the soft sighs of disbelief and pleasure that spilled past her lips.

Jack struggled to go slowly, but Mariah

thwarted him at every turn. She writhed in his arms as she responded to the darting taunts of his tongue and each tantalizing stroke of his fingertips. He sensed that she wanted to absorb him, and the depth of her desire served to escalate his own.

Jack finally gave in to her determination to destroy every shred of his restraint, hunger blazing in his heart for this woman. Tumbling her onto her back, he crouched over her, a magnificent male animal instinctively seeking his mate. He ran his fingertip from the delicate hollow of her throat to the valley between her high, full breasts. He cupped her breasts and flicked his thumbs back and forth across her nipples. They instantly hardened into tight nubs, as though begging for his mouth.

Mariah shivered, her breathing uneven and her body shifting seductively. She clutched at his thighs, her fingers kneading rhythmically, then edging higher. Jack froze as she trailed her knuckles across his lower abdomen and then combed her fingers through the thatch of dark curls that framed his maleness.

"You're amazing," he rasped. He struggled for control, when, in fact, he wanted to do nothing more than bury himself in the heated depths of her body.

Breathless, she met his gaze. Her back arched

when he leaned down and bathed the underside of each breast with his tongue. She groaned, arching yet again when he tugged at her nipples with his teeth.

Her hands found his shoulders, her fingers digging into his flesh, but it was the sweetest kind of lover's pain. Settling over her, his throbbing manhood poised between her parted thighs and his hands and fingers at her breasts, he claimed her mouth once more. The realization that he would never again find another woman like Mariah shot through him like an electrical charge.

He felt the inviting press of her pelvis as she tilted her hips beneath him, tempting him, luring him, seducing him until he feared that he might lose all control. Jack suddenly rolled onto his side, but Mariah followed him, turning into him, reaching blindly as she moaned her frustration. He brought her against him, his hand catching her at the hip. Sliding his narrow fingers between her legs, he dipped into the heat of her femininity, the delicate folds of moist flesh closing over his fingers as he slipped them into her body. She cried out, surging against his cupped hand, impaling herself even more, encouraging him with the sounds she made and the shifting of her body.

He delved deeply into the slick channel, his

lips and tongue simultaneously plundering her mouth. Her breasts plumped against his chest, her nipples rubbing against the hair that covered his chest. Her insides quivered and tightened at the intimacy of his touch. He drank in her gasps of disbelief, all the while pressing against the sensitive, swollen nub of flesh beneath his palm as his fingers stroked her heated depths.

Suddenly, shudders rocked Mariah's body and she tore her mouth from his and cried out. Holding her, Jack realized, was like trying to hold shattering crystal. Nothing could have prepared him for her responsiveness; no one could have grasped the pleasure that swept across him. He held her as she rode out the storm that consumed her. When her breathing calmed and her heartbeat slowed, he soothed her with gentle hands and tender kisses.

Rolling her onto her back a short while later, Jack shifted atop her, his body coiled with tension still unspent. Smoothing her long hair off her temples and away from her cheeks, he waited for Mariah to open her eyes.

Although he felt the excruciating strain of not plunging deeply into her body and seeking his own release, he wanted Mariah totally aware when he took her. He also needed to know that she was centered on the present, and that the past had no part in what they now shared.

Mariah exhaled softly, a dazed expression on her face when she finally opened her eyes and focused on him. "Incredible."

He smiled. "You're incredible."

She shook her head. "I meant you and the gift you just gave me."

Jack voiced his thoughts, although he had trouble coming to grips with even the possibility. "The first time?"

"Yes," she admitted, tears brimming in her eyes until she blinked them away. "The very first time."

Damn you to eternal hell, Darren, for cheating her, he thought. "There's more. Much more," he promised as he forced a smile to his lips and tried to banish from his mind the injustice of her life with a man undeserving of her gentle heart and passionate nature.

Mariah touched his cheek. He turned his head and kissed her fingertips. She trembled, drawing his gaze.

"Talk to me," he urged.

"What shall I say?"

"Tell me what you're thinking."

She glanced away. "My mind's a blank."

He frowned. "I don't believe you."

"I didn't expect to fall in love with you."

Stunned, he began, "Mariah—"

She pressed her fingertips against his lips to

keep him from speaking. "It's all right. You don't have to love me back. I just want you to know that you're loved."

Jack gathered her against his chest and held her, startled by her honesty and emotional courage, startled even more by the hunger that her words could arouse in his heart and soul. He wanted to hear them again, but he knew better than to tempt himself, knew better than to risk his emotions, and he knew better than to give Mariah false hope. She was a forever kind of woman, and he knew in his gut that she needed far more than he could ever offer her.

Burying his face in the curve that joined her neck and shoulder, he sipped at her skin, his senses basking in the scent and taste of her, his emotions torn as he tried not to want the love she offered. Mariah wrapped her arms around him, her head shifting to the left to expose more of her sensitive neck to his questing lips and teasing tongue. She moaned softly, the sound an echo of her desire. A single tear slid down her cheek.

He moved downward, tracing a path of ecstasy over her skin with his lips. He lingered at her breasts, alternating between the taut-tipped mounds. He teethed and tongued and suckled, his hands molding her swollen flesh until she arched like a drawn bow beneath him. Her slender legs stirred, her restlessness growing with what he knew was her escalating hunger for completion.

Jack shifted downward once again, his tongue darted flamelike strokes over her quivering belly, across each hipbone, and then her upper thighs.

Kneeling between her parted legs, he slid his hands beneath her hips and lifted her. Mariah lurched upward from the mattress. She reached for him, uncertainty shining in her eyes, but he shook his head.

"Jack . . ."

"Trust me."

"I do, but . . ."

"I want to give you heaven, and I need my own taste of it as well." He lowered his mouth to the silky cloud of pale hair that shielded her feminine secrets.

Mariah tumbled back against the pillows at the first flick of his tongue. When his mouth settled fully over her, Mariah gripped the bedding beneath her hands, stiffening briefly until she surrendered to the intimacy of his primitive caress. Her respiration grew more and more ragged while sensation cascaded through her like a never-ending waterfall. She moaned, the agonized sound one of mingled pleasure and disbelief.

Jack devastated her hold on reality, his clever tongue and mobile lips skimming, dipping, and tantalizing until Mariah nearly sobbed. He roused, he teased, and he taught her about the sensual generosity she'd been denied. And then he sent her spinning beyond the brink of rationality and control. She unraveled completely, the stunning force of her climax eclipsing her first experience as it moved outward from her core in ever-expanding waves to encompass her entire body.

Unable to hold back any longer, Jack gently lowered her hips to the mattress and surged up her body. He reached into the drawer of the nightstand beside his bed. Mariah continued to tremble with aftershocks as she lay sprawled beneath him.

A few moments later he gathered her shaking body into his arms. His embrace seemed to trigger some basic instinct within her, because she came alive beneath him almost instantly. Surprise swept through him as her hands moved feverishly up and down his back.

"Now, please," she said raggedly when she gripped his hips and trapped his engorged manhood between her thighs. "I need you now, Jack. Inside me."

He sank into her with one smooth thrust. Despite the agony it caused him, he immediately stilled his movements and allowed Mariah to adjust to his deep penetration.

She felt tight, hot, and slick, like the heaven that he had promised to her. Jack's already tenuous control disintegrated as her flesh quivered and tightened around him. He thrust into her, over and over again, instinct taking command of his consciousness, his senses so alive they burned like live coals deep within the core of him. He felt more alive and more cared for than he had in years as Mariah clung to him.

The sensual madness that seized them both seemed to last forever.

Jack succumbed totally to Mariah, driving into her, repeatedly, thoroughly, his need and desire untamed now. Slick with sweat, he felt Mariah match him stroke for stroke. She gasped his name, her fingers pressing into his lower back as she urged him on.

He grabbed her hands, lifted them above her head, and held them there. Palm to palm, he loomed over her, plunging into her, his gaze locked on her face.

They watched each other, amazement and love in Mariah's eyes, adoration in Jack's as he drove into her, his pace steadily accelerating, his muscular body shuddering and rippling with tension.

She whispered her love, and his heart swelled with emotions. She moaned suddenly, then arched beneath him. Seconds later she came apart with a little scream that electrified him.

Jack felt the tremors that ripped through her like tiny convulsions. Her climax sent him over the edge, flinging him into the embrace of a swirling kaleidoscope of sensation. He exploded inside her. Nothing in his life had prepared him for the fiery tumult that seized him and held him for several heart-stopping moments.

He sagged suddenly, sapped of energy and unable to breathe. Sprawled across her, Jack eventually mustered the energy to shift them onto their sides.

Jack didn't know what to think anymore, so he told himself to stop thinking. Easier said than done, he realized a few minutes later, after his mind had wandered through the possibilities of what it would be like to be loved every day of his life by Mariah Chandler. He swore, the harsh word erupting from him.

Mariah stirred in his arms and lifted her head to peer at him. "What?" she asked, confusion in her eyes.

He gently tucked her head beneath his chin. "Nothing, Vassar. Go back to sleep."

Sighing contentedly, she snuggled even closer. Jack automatically tightened his embrace, his instincts refusing to honor the common-sense assertions being made by his brain.

He closed his eyes and savored the simple pleasure of holding Mariah and listening to the sound of her breathing as she fell asleep in his arms. He told himself that he'd deal with reality in the bright light of day, but no sooner. He needed this time, this illusion that happiness with this particular woman was within reach. Their lives, he knew, would take them in opposite directions soon enough. Then the illusion would end and the fantasy would die.

Jack replaced the telephone receiver and joined Mariah at the breakfast table early the next morning. "The car rental agency is arranging a replacement for you. It'll be delivered to the cottage in a couple of hours."

She set aside her coffee cup. "Good. I've got a packed schedule today."

"And tonight?"

She grinned at him. Extending her hand across the top of the table, she welcomed the press of his palm over hers. "Do you have any ideas?"

Jack laughed. He loved seeing her this way. She reminded him of a sexy kitten, all warm and playful, an image, he realized, that wasn't at all at odds with the sophisticated and very capable woman of the world who managed the affairs of a national charitable foundation. She was the most versatile woman he'd ever known, and he sensed that only a fool would attempt to categorize her as anything less. Jack McMillan did not consider himself a fool.

"Well?"

"I might be able to think of something," he conceded.

"If you don't, I will."

"I have every confidence in you, Vassar."

Mariah squeezed his hand and then picked up her coffee cup, her gaze traveling to the window a few feet from where they sat. A stream wound lazily through the dense foliage that shaded the area behind Jack's home. It all seemed serene and quite removed from the busy coastal community of Santa Barbara. Mariah sighed, content as she sipped her coffee and enjoyed the quiet early-morning hours with Jack. Clad in one of his T-shirts, her face free of makeup, and her hair woven into a loose braid, she felt utterly carefree.

"What do you expect of me, Mariah Chandler?"

Startled by his unexpected question, she glanced at him. Her smile faded when she saw the seriousness of his expression. Sensing the importance of her reply, Mariah lowered her cup to the table and chose her words with care. "Only what you can freely give."

"Are you sure?"

"Yes," she whispered.

"I'll disappoint you if you expect too much of me," he warned. "You should also know that I'm not in the market for a permanent relationship."

"Most men aren't." She knew she sounded flip, but she didn't feel that way.

"You deserve better. You don't want to settle for someone like me."

She forced herself to her feet. "I'll let you know when I'm bored with you. Fair enough?"

He grabbed her arm as she started to walk past him. "You won't get bored."

"Then we don't need to have this conversation quite yet, do we? And you definitely don't have to go to the trouble of determining what's best for me."

"Last night—"

"Was the most extraordinary night of my life. Let me enjoy it for a little while longer before you smack me in the face with reality. All right?"

His jaw tight, he nodded and removed his hand from her arm. Mariah walked to the sink and rinsed out her coffee cup. As she leaned against the counter and tried to control her disappointment, she sensed that Jack's past had come back to haunt him again.

She felt compassion for him, because she understood better than most people just how crippling painful memories could be. But she also felt protective of what they'd shared the previous night, and she experienced a moment of pure frustration that he seemed to need to diminish it.

She heard his chair scrape across the tile floor. Straightening, she prepared herself for his next comment, whatever it might be. He surprised her when he simply placed his hands on her shoulders. He was underestimating her ability to cope with the secrets of his past. And that made her even more determined now to help him come to terms with it once and for all.

"I honestly don't want to hurt you," he said as he pulled her back against him and filled his hands with her breasts.

Mariah shivered beneath his sensual touch, loving the possessive feel of his hands on her body. She turned in the circle of his arms and looked up at him. She needed to see his face, especially his eyes. They were the proverbial windows to Jack McMillan's wounded soul.

"If you don't want to hurt me, then don't push me away," she suggested quietly.

"I don't want to, Vassar, but you have to know the truth."

"I'm a big girl."

"You're a lot more than that."

Mariah saw the regret that tinged his smile. "I certainly hope so."

"Trust me, you are."

"I'll trust you when you're doing what I think is right. Otherwise, I'll trust myself and my instincts."

"Have I just been put on some kind of notice?" he asked, his gaze suddenly wary.

Mariah nodded. She wanted his love, and she would fight for him, but she wasn't a biddable creature who lacked the ability or the will to think for herself.

"I'm in way over my head with you, aren't I?"

She shrugged. "Maybe you've just never known anyone like me before."

"I haven't," he said, certainty ringing in his voice.

"But you do now," she pointed out as she reached up and laced her fingers together behind his neck. Guiding his head down, she rose up on tiptoes and tenderly kissed him. Mariah slipped out of his arms in the next heartbeat.

Jack didn't follow her. Leaning against the edge of the counter, he simply watched her as she came to a stop in the middle of the large kitchen and turned to look at him. "You've got something else on your mind, so why don't you just say it and get it over with."

She wasn't at all surprised by his ability to

read her emotions. He'd done it so many times in the last two months, she'd lost count. As she stared at him Mariah tried to determine the best way to present her plans for the mansion. In the end, she simply revealed the facts. "I intend to use the mansion as a shelter once it's completed. It will be named after my grandmother, and privately funded by her estate."

"Why didn't you tell me before?"

"I thought you hated me at the beginning, and I didn't want Chandler House treated as a potential institution."

"I never hated you, and it wouldn't have been."

"I apologize for not being more forthcoming, but I didn't want anyone working on the project to think of it as anything but a home, because that's what it will be."

"This isn't a surprise," he remarked.

"It isn't?" Mariah frowned. "It should be, since no one knew my intentions."

"The wallpaper has arrived."

Confused, she gave him a blank look. "Pardon me?"

"The wallpaper," Jack said again.

Mariah grinned, finally understanding his comment. "You've seen the wallpaper for the playrooms and some of the bedrooms?"

Jack nodded. "I put the puzzle together last

night after listening to your comments about the shortage of shelters."

"I waited too long to tell you," she confessed. "I've been feeling very guilty."

"You're forgiven."

She smiled. Jack pushed away from the counter and crossed the kitchen. Mariah watched him, unable to discern his intentions.

Pausing in front of her, Jack took her hands and tugged her forward. She looked faintly bemused as she stepped closer. Cupping her hips with his hands, he lifted her up and against him. The khaki shorts he wore failed to conceal his hardening loins.

Breathless, she slid her arms around his neck and her legs around his narrow waist. "What exactly are you doing?" While her heart raced she waited for his answer.

Jack nibbled at her lips, then bathed her full lower lip with the tip of his tongue. "You," he finally answered, his eyes dark with desire.

Her senses sparkled like diamonds. "You're doing *me*?"

"Precisely."

She blinked as she grasped his meaning. "Now?"

"Shut up," he advised gently.

"All right," she managed just before he took her mouth and thoroughly plundered it.

Jack eventually carried her back to his bed. As he stepped out of his shorts Mariah asked, "Does this mean you approve of my plans?"

Stripping off her T-shirt, he sank down over her, his gaze locked on her face, his hands cupping her breasts, and his manhood poised at the entrance to her body.

"I approve, Vassar. I definitely approve."

TEN

Jack and Mariah were rarely apart in the weeks that followed. They spent their days at the mansion and nearly all of their nights together at Jack's home. She brought color and energy into every facet of his life. Her passion, her laughter, and her intelligence fascinated him, and he couldn't get enough of her.

She taught him about gentleness with every gesture and every word. He took her on explosively sensual journeys that left her gasping and weak with pleasure. She gave him the gift of her love while he tried to convince himself that he wasn't falling in love with her. She didn't press him about his past, even though he knew it bothered her not to understand some of the choices he'd made in his life.

They shared lively conversations in which he

respected her opinions even if he didn't agree with them. In her defense of her viewpoints, he glimpsed the courage that it had taken for her to move beyond the cowering passivity that Darren had forced her to learn.

She blended into his life, his heart, and his consciousness as though specifically designed for him. Jack felt himself growing dangerously content. To counter his feelings, he anticipated the day when the fantasy would end and reality would send him crashing back to earth. The anticipation gnawed at him at unexpected moments, and his conscience told him that he was the worst kind of fool for being willing to give up a woman like Mariah Chandler.

The intimacy they shared, both emotional and physical, made him even more aware of the loneliness he'd experienced in recent years, and it prompted thoughts of what it would be like not to live the lone-wolf existence he'd chosen for himself. Jack consciously fought the temptation Mariah posed by reminding himself that she would return to Washington once the work on Chandler House was complete. Still, he savored her presence in his life, too hungry for her to be noble or to admit to her that a future together wasn't possible.

The restoration of the mansion moved forward on schedule. The more intricate trim and moldings for the windows and walls were being installed now that the walls had been bolted into place and the ceilings and floors finished. A local decorator orchestrated the wallpapering and painting of the upper floors after the new plumbing had been installed. Cabinets were completed and fitted into place in the playrooms, library, kitchen, and pantry.

Jack gave his crew high marks for respecting his privacy, but the absence of comment about the change in his attitude toward Mariah didn't fool him. He saw approval in the facial expressions of his men. Although their behavior amazed him at times, he appreciated their attempts to encourage his relationship with Mariah, especially when José's garden became the source of bouquets of flowers that found their way to the front seat of Jack's truck and when several of the men arranged a picnic lunch for two, complete with crystal and linen napkins, in the newly constructed gazebo.

Mariah convinced him to hire a nurse for Tommy once his parents checked him out of the hospital. They visited the apprentice carpenter, signed his cast, and discovered that he'd proposed marriage to his flame-haired nurse— several times, in fact. The young woman refused to take him seriously, which seemed to amaze her patient and prompted Mariah to predict laughingly that Tommy would pursue her all the way to the altar.

The weeks turned into a month. Jack felt as though he walked an emotional tightrope as the restoration entered its final phase. Frustrated and edgy, he left the mansion earlier than usual one afternoon and drove to the battered women's shelter in Santa Barbara, where he'd arranged to meet Mariah.

He arrived twenty minutes early and decided to ease the tension he felt by taking a walk while he waited for Mariah. He wandered through the parklike setting that formed a border around the complex, pausing when he heard the sound of childish laughter. Glancing beyond the chain-link fence that surrounded the play yard, Jack spotted Mariah.

He stopped dead in his tracks, his heart turning to a chunk of lead as he watched her. She sat beneath the shade of an oak tree, a group of small children gathered around her and two toddlers seated in her lap as she read them a story. Mariah reminded him of a dream he'd once had, the dream of a happy marriage to a loving partner, the dream of having children to love and nurture.

Gripping the top of the fence with both hands, he recalled how, during their courtship, his ex-wife had insisted that she shared his desire for children. Fool that he'd been, he'd taken her at her word, not discovering her real feelings until several years later. He felt sick inside as memories played out in his mind.

Jack remembered his rage when he'd stumbled over the bills for Delia's abortion. He remembered his shock that she hadn't bothered to reveal her pregnancy to him. She lied, telling him that she'd been billed in error for someone else's medical care. He'd believed her—had forced himself to—but he discovered the truth when he happened to be paired in a golf tournament with the doctor who'd performed the surgery. The pain he felt kept him silent for almost a week, but his anger festered and grew.

He remembered tearing apart their bedroom and bathroom, some gut instinct telling him that she'd lied before and that he'd been lying to himself for years just to have her in his life. He finally found the birth-control pills she'd been taking on the sly for their entire marriage.

Jack closed his eyes, but he still heard the haunting echo of her voice as she denied her duplicity. He saw her phony tears of dismay as she insisted that she needed the abortion for health reasons and was too upset by the situation to discuss it with him. He pressed her, wanting everything to be out in the open at last.

He recalled the exact moment when the real

Delia had emerged, the haughty, self-serving creature who declared that she had no intention of ruining her figure by having a baby. She'd stood toe to toe with him in their living room, shouting her admission in the face of his fury that she'd never intended to become pregnant. She delivered another crippling blow just moments later. Out of control, she told him that he hadn't fathered the baby, so he should be happy that she'd resolved her little problem.

Jack remembered grabbing for her, remembered wanting to shake her. She ran from him then, out of their multimillion-dollar home, and, ultimately, out of his life. She'd gone too far, and in a moment of lucidity when she glanced over her shoulder at him, she seemed to realize it, although by that point he hadn't really cared. The damage was done, the marriage destroyed. Her revelations sent him staggering through a mine field of disbelief and betrayal.

After a two-week alcohol binge, he accepted that his ten-year marriage had been a sham from start to finish. He went through the motions of life for almost a month, his emotions frozen and his creative instincts dulled. He initiated divorce proceedings and sold the successful architectural firm he'd founded. Delia delivered her final blow in a meeting in his lawyer's office. Angry with the proposed divorce settlement, she revealed the identity of the man who'd gotten her pregnant.

Jack quickly ended the negotiations. He simply gave her everything she asked for, signed all the documents, and walked away from the debris of his life. He never went back, nor did he look back, and he never spoke of what had happened to another person. He decided then that happiness was too fleeting an emotion to pursue, no matter how lonely he might become and no matter how much he loved any woman.

"Have you been waiting long?" Mariah asked as she walked up to Jack a little while later.

He jerked in surprise, as though coming out of a trance. The fence rattled. Jack loosened his grip on it and took a step backward before he met her gaze.

Mariah's smile faded the instant she saw the strained expression on his face. A chill swept over her. "Jack, is something wrong?"

"Nothing's wrong."

His voice was raspy, and she sensed that something terrible had happened. In the past she would have fled a man in this condition, but Jack never lost control and she trusted him too much even to think that he might. "You aren't ill, are you? Is everyone all right at Chandler House?"

"I'm fine, and they're fine," he said, sounding remote yet in pain. "Are you ready to leave?"

"Of course. Why don't we go home now?"

Jack frowned, and Mariah didn't understand why. She decided not to press him. Whatever was wrong, she preferred the privacy of his home for personal conversations. "Shall I drive? You look tired. I'm glad it's Friday. I think we could both use some rest."

She slipped her hand into his as they made their way to his car. He gripped her hand so tightly that her fingers started to tingle.

Jack held the passenger door open for her, and she didn't challenge his decision to get behind the wheel. Although preoccupied, he drove home without incident.

They walked into the kitchen together. Mariah placed her purse on the kitchen table and stepped out of her shoes. She turned when she felt Jack's hand on her shoulder.

She saw pain and disillusionment in his hazel eyes, and the sight of such anguish made her ache inside. "Talk to me, please."

He gripped her shoulder. "I need you."

Unprepared for his comment, she stared at him.

"I need you now, Mariah."

She nodded, moving into his arms without hesitation. Jack, she knew, didn't normally use a word like *need*. It seemed almost foreign to his vocabulary. *Want* was more his style, because needing anyone or anything smacked of weakness and dependence to someone like him. The expression on his face told her clearly that he did need her, probably more than he'd ever needed anyone in his life. That he felt such intense vulnerability made her tremble with worry over him.

He shuddered as he put his arms around her. She pressed against him, sharing her strength and her compassion by simply returning his embrace. His arousal stimulated her, and she shivered with desire as her body softened and heated.

He lifted her into his arms and held her against his chest. As she looped her arms around his neck Mariah absorbed the tension that thrummed through his body like a live current. She held tightly to him, protective feelings washing through her as he made his way down the hallway.

He carried her into his bedroom, then lowered her to stand beside the bed. He watched her, his eyes locked on her face as he jerked open his shirt, the buttons scattering across the floor, and stripped off his jeans and shorts. Mariah hastily shed her own clothing, willing to follow his lead, desperate for any clue that would help her understand his frame of mind.

Still silent, he gathered her against his tautly muscled body, a strangled groan escaping him when she brought her arms up and around his shoulders and molded herself to him. They fell across the bed, landing on their sides.

Facing each other, they breathed unsteadily. Swiftly tipping her onto her back, Jack positioned himself over her, his legs bent at the knees so that his muscled thighs bracketed her hips. He shifted against her, his manhood nudging at her belly and reminding her yet again of his potent maleness and his skill as a lover.

She kept her eyes on his face, trying to read the emotions in his shadowed expression even as she reached for him. Taking him into her hands, she caressed him until he shook from her touch, his eyes fell closed, and he bowed his head as he struggled for control. "You don't have to hold back. Just tell me what you want," she urged, her hands traveling intimately over him. "Anything I have to give is yours. Anything."

Leaning forward a few moments later, Jack framed her face with shaking hands and whispered against her lips, "Love me, Mariah. Please just love me for now."

"I do," Mariah whispered, almost weeping because he didn't seem to realize just how deeply she did love him. "And I always will, even after you send me away."

He flinched as though she'd struck him. Lifting her hands to his shoulders, she tried to soothe him, tried to help him deal with whatever was causing him so much pain.

Jack took her mouth, his tongue plunging deeply, exploring every curve and ridge. Then he sucked at her tongue, drew it into his mouth, and teased the tip with his teeth. He staked his claim on her, thoroughly, aggressively, and she tasted that claiming, that mark of possession along with his hunger and his passion, but she tasted something more, something wounded and vulnerable.

She returned his kiss, making her own incendiary statement of possession. Reaching between their bodies once again, she expressed her love with her provocatively skimming fingertips. She inhaled his groans as she simultaneously stroked and cupped him. He jerked beneath her hands, his sex reminding her of a length of satin-covered steel that pulsed with life. She stirred restlessly beneath him as she crossed the invisible boundary line between desire and a soul-deep craving to mate.

When Mariah thought she couldn't stand it any longer, Jack relinquished her mouth and knelt between her thighs. She watched him, her breath catching as his fingers fanned over her lower abdomen, his thumbs stroking along the seam of her silk-covered secrets. Exquisite sensations tremored through her entire body. Mariah gasped softly, then moaned as he parted her and found the moisture glistening there.

She extended her arms in the same instant that he glanced up at her. "Jack, please, I need you too."

Suddenly all primitive male, he surged up her body and penetrated her in one long, smooth lunge of muscular power. She cried out at the intense pleasure he gave her. He speared into her repeatedly, his pace harder, faster than ever before. There was a recklessness to his love-making, and Mariah greeted it and him with a wildly uninhibited response of her own.

Need dominated his every move. Need drove her to respond to each thrust with an equally forceful counterthrust. Need mapped the explosively passionate route they followed. And need determined the outcome.

They reached their summits within seconds of each other, the stunning climaxes leaving them spent, gasping for air, and sweat-covered as they collapsed in a tangle of limbs.

Jack rolled them onto their sides. She rested her head on his shoulder and placed her hand over his heart as he held her, the only sound in the room their ragged breathing.

In the aftermath of their stormy joining, Mariah waited patiently for Jack to speak, but he disappointed her. He held her, instead, never once during that tempestuous night that ensued allowing her to leave his side, but he kept to himself whatever was troubling him. Mariah couldn't help wondering as she drifted off to sleep why he felt so reluctant to confide in the one person who loved him enough to worry about him and to share his burdens.

The next morning, while she stood in the shower, Mariah realized that they'd neglected to use any protection at all during the previous night. Because of Jack's reflective mood over breakfast a little while later, she kept that fact to herself. Whatever the consequences, she knew that she would deal with them without a single moment of regret.

With the crew taking a much-deserved Saturday off and Jack at his office in downtown Santa Barbara for an early meeting, Mariah discovered that the mansion was hers to explore at her leisure that morning. She strolled through the second- and third-story bedrooms and bathrooms for nearly an hour, her pleasure mounting as she inspected the progress made by the decorator and her helpers. With nearly half of the rooms completed, Mariah felt a profound sense of satisfaction.

She made her way down the restored staircase to the first floor, running her fingers along the carved banister that Jack had labored over.

She walked to the kitchen, her gaze traveling over the shining brass fixtures at the oversized sink, the washed white cabinets that lined the walls, and the pale rose tile that topped the counters and covered the floors. As she stood there she couldn't help wondering what Emma would have thought of Jackson McMillan Wainright III. Mariah smiled, picturing the two of them going nose to nose over an issue, any issue, and taking opposide sides just for the sake of challenging each other. They would have liked and respected each other, she decided.

Glancing up when she heard footsteps coming down the front hallway, Mariah's smile widened to a grin. *Think of the man, and he suddenly appears.* "I'm in the kitchen," she called out. Turning to greet him, she stiffened when she recognized the short, paunchy man who stood in the kitchen doorway.

Mariah reacted instinctively. She darted toward the backdoor. As she grabbed the doorknob a large hand slammed against the wood above her head. Despite her racing heart and hammering pulse, she went perfectly still, calming herself with effort, reminding herself that to show fear in the face of a threat was an invitation for that threat to be intensified.

His physical strength was superior to hers. She knew it, and she decided to deal with it. Turning, she looked at Richard Hilton.

He scowled at her, recognition in his pale, anger-filled eyes. "Going somewhere?" he asked.

"I was planning to leave."

"No, you aren't, you bitch. You're not going anywhere until you listen to what I have to say to you."

"I said everything I had to say in court, Mr. Hilton. I doubt that anything we say to each other now will be of much value to either one of us."

"What the hell are you doing here? You aren't one of Jack's people. I'd know if you were."

"I own Chandler House, but that isn't important, is it?"

"You rich bitch," he seethed. "Your money won't protect you now. You lied about me, and nobody gets away with lying about Rich Hilton."

"Did I lie? I don't think so. I was at the shelter the night you broke in and attacked your wife, and we both know that I'm the person who called the authorities. I told the judge what I witnessed, nothing more, so what is it exactly that you want from me now?" she asked. Drawing in a shallow breath, she thought of her long-ago vow never to be intimidated by anyone or anything ever again.

"You're damn right I want something from you, lady. I want my wife and kids back, and I want them back now."

"I don't think that's going to happen. Your wife is divorcing you."

"Only because you talked her into it. If you and people like you hadn't interfered, we'd be fine."

She loathed the whine that had crept into his voice, because she recognized it for what it was. Self-pity that invariably led to the justification of any action he took, no matter how reckless or violent. "They weren't *fine*, Mr. Hilton, and you aren't *fine*. You're an angry man, and you take out your anger on innocent people. I overheard your attorney when he advised you to get help. It doesn't appear that you took his advice."

He grabbed at her suddenly. Mariah tried to duck beyond his reach, but he seized her wrists and dragged her across the kitchen. He released her, but only to extend his arms as he began advancing on her again.

Mariah took a step backward, then another. Richard Hilton kept moving forward, finally backing her into a corner. She lifted her chin and glared at him. She smelled the alcohol that tainted his skin. "Why are you really here?" she asked quietly.

He frowned, as though momentarily baffled by her question. "I came to see Jack. He usually works on Saturday."

Keep him off balance, she told herself as she slowly slipped the fingers of her right hand into her pocket until she touched the stun gun. She thought for a moment about Darren. She'd lost count of the number of times that he'd backed her against a wall, towering over her, his fists raised and ready to strike. She hated the memories almost as much as she'd hated the man.

"Where is he?" Hilton shouted.

"Jack's not here yet, but he will be shortly." Mariah glanced at her watch, making a show of her desire to help Hilton. "I expect him anytime. We have a meeting scheduled for this morning."

His beady eyes narrowed to slits. "You're lying."

She shrugged, giving him a sample of the negligent heiress who had money to burn and time to waste. "I don't lie, Mr. Hilton. I don't need to."

"I'm gonna make you pay, lady."

Anger suddenly ruined her facade of calm. "The same way you made your wife and children pay?" she demanded. When she saw that he looked genuinely shocked by her gall, Mariah almost laughed in his face. Instead, she sighed as though supremely bored by him and his trivial concerns. "I really think you should leave now."

He grabbed her shoulders, his fingers digging into her as he shook her and then slammed her back against the wall. "And I think you should shut your trap. I don't like what comes out of it."

Her hand still in her pocket, Mariah gripped the gun in the palm of her hand and loosened the safety catch with her thumb. "I know how to defend myself, Mr. Hilton. Do you really want to continue this conversation?"

"Don't try to con me, lady. I'll do any damn thing I want."

"I think you're making a very serious mistake. Shall I prove it to you?" she asked, fury rising inside her like a tidal wave as she started to withdraw her hand from her pocket.

"Mariah."

Her name sounded like a growl from a predatory animal. She blinked in surprise, then glanced past Hilton. Jack stood in the kitchen doorway, his fists clenched, and on his face a look of primal rage that made Hilton's anger pale in comparison, eclipsing anything she'd ever seen before.

Hilton followed her gaze, his eyes widening

with shock. Jack bolted across the room, grabbed the electrician by the scruff of the neck, and threw him onto the floor. Hilton slid several feet, slammed into a cabinet, and slumped over onto his face.

"I'm all right, Jack," she insisted as she shoved the gun back into her pocket and then seized his arm with both hands. He tugged free, his gaze darting between Mariah and Hilton, who lay sprawled on the floor. "Really, Jack. Don't waste your time on him. He's a bully and nothing more."

"Why did that son of . . ." He breathed in deeply, then exhaled slowly. After eyeing Hilton, he turned to Mariah. "What the hell happened?"

"I testified against him in family court after he broke into the shelter and attacked his wife. He's been terrorizing Adele and the children for years. She finally decided to leave him, and he holds me responsible for the fact that she's seeking a divorce. When he found me here this morning and realized I was alone, he decided that he wanted a little revenge."

"He was assaulting you," Jack gritted out, ruddy color staining his cheeks as he checked her over from head to foot.

Mariah shook her head. "He spent most of his time trying to intimidate me. There's a difference. And for the record, his tactics didn't work."

"Why are you so blasted calm? Any other woman would be—" He broke off when Hilton groaned and tried to get to his knees. "Stay here while I take out the garbage."

Jack hauled a still-shaken Hilton out of the kitchen, down the front hallway, and out onto the verandah. Mariah followed, wanting to make certain that Jack's temper didn't get the best of him. She watched him shove the man off the porch.

"Don't come back, Hilton. Ever. Close down your business, because you'll never work for me or any other contractor in the county again. Find another place to live while you're at it. Try an uninhabited island, because if I hear even a rumor that you've threatened another woman or child again, I will personally make it my life's work to see that you rot in jail."

Hilton scrambled to his van, which was soon screeching out of the front yard.

Jack turned to find Mariah standing behind him. She absently rubbed her wrists as she gazed up at him, a faint smile on her face.

"Are you on some kind of medication?" he asked, obviously still confused by her calmness.

She laughed out loud at his ludicrous question, although she understood why he asked it. She walked into Jack's embrace, a mild case of the shakes making her cling to him for a long moment. When she finally lifted her face from his chest, she mumbled, "Sorry. Delayed reaction."

Jack tightened his hold on her. "I'd still like to tear that sorry bastard limb from limb. He shouldn't have touched you."

"There's no need." She smiled, suddenly aware of the value of her confrontation with Richard Hilton. "I wasn't afraid."

Jack frowned. "Explain yourself, Vassar."

"I was not afraid of that man. He made me angry, very angry, but that was all."

"You seem surprised that you can handle yourself in a crisis."

"I haven't been tested before, not this way."

He nodded, understanding. As she stepped back from him he noticed her wrists. Red from Hilton's rough handling, they ached a little, but that was all.

"He got careless as he was dragging me across the kitchen."

A muscle ticked in his jaw. "You'll have bruises," he observed, his voice ragged.

"They'll fade."

"We need to get you some ice."

Mariah tugged one hand free, reached up, and cupped the side of his face with her open palm. "I'm fine. Quit worrying."

"Ice," he said. "Or I take you to the emergency room for X rays."

"Ice," she conceded. "My place?"

He scooped her up into his arms and carried her to his truck. He settled her in the front seat.

"My purse and car keys are in the kitchen."

"We'll get them later." He paused, studying her with unexpected intensity in his hazel eyes. "I would have killed him if he'd hurt you. I wouldn't have been able to stop myself."

Mariah pressed her fingertips against his lips. She didn't want to hear him talking this way. "He's gone, so stop thinking about what happened. It's over, and he won't be back."

Jack drove her to her cottage and opened the front door with the keys she'd given him several weeks earlier. He filled a bowl with ice and made her submerge her wrist in it.

Mariah let him fuss over her. She knew it made him feel better, and she realized that even if he couldn't bring himself to express his feelings for her, he cared enough to worry about her. It wasn't a declaration of love, but it was something tangible to hold on to.

ELEVEN

Following the incident with Richard Hilton, Jack spoke to his crew in private. He asked them to keep an eye on Mariah. He gave them few details other than that Hilton had behaved inappropriately around her. The expressions of outrage on their faces assured him that she wouldn't have to worry if Hilton approached her at the mansion.

Hilton's behavior forced him to reevaluate every aspect of his relationship with Mariah, not just how he would spend his future. Alone and bitter, or partnered with a vital woman who possessed more courage and resilience than ten people combined. He loved her, more deeply than anything or anyone in his life. She embodied a passion for life that he craved, and because she was crucial to his happiness, he vowed to move beyond his past. He knew he would die inside if he didn't.

As he came to terms with the betrayal that had haunted him for ten long years, Jack pulled back emotionally from Mariah in the weeks that followed, his behavior self-protective, his attitude reflective, and his brooding silences endless. He spent his days at home or at his downtown office, leaving most of the final details of the restoration to Mariah and his crew. When he did go to the mansion, it was at the end of the day, when he could work and think in private.

He didn't deliberately set out to hurt Mariah, but he saw bewilderment in her eyes and felt her dismay. He didn't know how she managed it, but she weathered the silent war he waged with himself. She remained patient and caring, although they rarely talked and made love only in the predawn hours when he couldn't keep himself from reaching out to her and expressing physically what his heart refused to allow him to say.

It took him time, but he accepted the reality that his departure from Washington had done nothing more than delay his recovery from Delia's betrayal. Jack slowly came to terms with the lie he'd lived for nearly ten years, his heart and his emotions frozen in time. He longed now for the peace of mind and the happiness that had always seemed so fleeting. He'd found those things, and so much more, with Mariah, but he'd been too thickheaded to see it or to trust her. She'd reached out to him in spite of his stubbornness, a catalyst to his healing, a balm to his battered emotions. She'd thawed the ice that encased his heart and reawakened him to the luxury of feeling positive emotions and loving without reserve or restraint.

Having tested her patience in the extreme, Jack understood when she finally lost her temper one morning. "I've had enough of your moodiness, Jack," she announced. "I want and deserve more than sex from you. When you're finished with whatever it is that you're doing to yourself, give me a call and we'll talk."

He watched her drive away. He'd seen the tears he'd caused, and didn't blame her for leaving or attempt to stop her. He needed time to find a solution to the miles that would separate them once she returned to Washington and the Chandler Foundation headquarters. Life without Mariah was no longer an option, so he promised himself that he would find a compromise that wouldn't jeopardize their professional commitments.

Late one evening Jack found a note on his drafting table from José, informing him that Mariah had just returned from a three-day trip to Washington. He already knew, just as he knew the reason for the trip in the first place. Because he worried about her, he'd monitored her schedule through Vivian Witherspoon, queried José and his men about her activities at the mansion, and driven past the cottage late each night to make certain that she was safe behind a closed door.

Jack decided that this was the night to talk to her, to put the past to rest once and for all and to embrace the future. As he finished sanding the fireplace mantel in the mansion's library, he planned what he would say to her and prayed she would listen. He also prayed that she would want to share the future with him.

Jackson McMillan Wainright III promised himself that he would never again make Mariah pay for another woman's duplicitous nature. He also vowed to reclaim his identity as an architect and to resume his position as the heir and chief operating officer of one of the largest family-founded manufacturing concerns ever established in the state of Virginia—his late father's legacy, the same legacy that Jack had left in the hands of others for many years.

Living a lie no longer appealed to him.

Mariah heard the fire engine sirens as they screamed into the night, the eerie sound moving closer and closer and increasing her fear for Jack. She knew his schedule as well as she knew her own name. He worked at the mansion until late into the night, nearly every night now.

Stepping into her shoes, she grabbed her car keys and dashed outside. She arrived at the mansion less than two minutes later, and the sight that greeted her filled her with apprehension.

Several large fire trucks and an ambulance cluttered the front yard. Men moved around the perimeter of the building, speaking into hand-held radios under the glare of portable lighting that turned the night into day. Mariah raced to the ambulance and peered into the back of it. Relieved that no one was there, she turned, desperate to find someone who would tell her what had happened.

She scanned the front of the mansion and the roofline, but saw no evidence of fire damage, even though she smelled the pungent odor of smoke. It seemed tainted with another smell, but she couldn't place it, and she immediately forgot her curiosity when she spotted Jack being guided down the side of the house by a paramedic. Although he was walking on his own, his hands were wrapped in gauze.

She ran forward, meeting him and the paramedic as they paused near the verandah railing. With his face soot-marked and his clothes equally filthy, he looked exhausted and frustrated. Mariah controlled the impulse to throw herself into his arms. Considering the expression on his face, she doubted that he'd appreciate her worry, let alone welcome the love that motivated her. Instead, she struggled for a calm she didn't feel before asking, "Are you all right?"

He jerked a nod in her direction. "The mansion's fine. The damage is confined to the back porch behind the kitchen."

She clenched her teeth in frustration. "That isn't what I asked you."

The paramedic responded to her distress. "He'll be all right, ma'am. No permanent damage, just blisters, a few abrasions, and minor smoke inhalation. But he shouldn't try to use his hands for a few days."

"Thank you. Should I take him to the emergency room?"

"He says he doesn't want to go."

"He'll go if you think it would be wise to have him checked over by a physician."

"*He* isn't going anywhere except home," Jack said impatiently, his temper flaring.

Mariah didn't dignify his comment with a response.

"If you don't have sterile gauze pads on hand, I can give you a supply," offered the paramedic as he looked sympathetically at Mariah.

"We'd appreciate that." She ignored Jack's scowl.

Mariah accepted the sealed plastic packets the paramedic gave her. "Can the fire department handle everything from now on, or does someone need to speak to me before we leave? I own the mansion."

The paramedic summoned a man whose uniform indicated that he was in charge of the firefighting detail. Mariah supplied him with her phone number, the keys to the doors of the mansion that she kept on her key ring, and accepted his business card. Once they arranged for a meeting and a daylight inspection of the site of the fire, she excused herself. Mariah found Jack slouched against the front of his truck.

He straightened as she approached him. "The mobile phone's on the front seat. I need to call José."

She glanced at his gauze wrapped hands. "I'll call him later."

"I want him out here tonight."

"What happened?" she asked.

"An electrical fire."

She paled, her thoughts speeding to the one person who'd threatened her more than once with reprisals for her interference in his life. "Richard Hilton?"

"It could have been. I'll deal with him myself if he's responsible for this. This would have been a nightmare if it had happened when the place was filled with women and children."

"We need all the wiring rechecked, don't we?"

Jack nodded. "I'll have José handle it."

"I intend to file charges if Hilton had anything to do with this. I don't care if he does get himself into counseling."

"You won't have any other choice if the arson investigator can prove a connection. The lock on the porch door was jimmied, so they're dusting for prints."

Mariah nodded. "Where are your keys?"

He half turned. "My right back pocket."

She dug for them. She noticed then that the soot covering his clothes was denser than she'd first realized, and he reeked of smoke. After removing his briefcase and mobile phone, Mariah locked the truck. Jack walked with her to the Mercedes.

"You okay?" Jack asked as she opened the passenger door for him.

"I'm not sure. I wasn't exactly prepared for this. I don't think I know how I feel right now."

"I guess you heard the sirens."

She nodded. As she drove back to the cottage she glanced at Jack several times. He was stone-faced, his features seemingly cast in granite. Nothing new about that, she reminded herself.

They walked into the cottage, and Mariah dropped Jack's briefcase, his mobile phone, and her purse on the couch. "You need a shower. I think you left a change of clothes in the closet the . . . the last time you were here overnight."

"I'm thirsty."

"Would you like a beer, or maybe something stronger?"

"Brandy, please. Why don't we share one?"

She met his gaze. She saw something unexpected in his eyes. Appreciation, she thought, and for a moment she didn't know how to respond. Pondering Jack's behavior in recent weeks as she poured an inch of brandy into a snifter, Mariah didn't know what to say to him. He'd let her leave him, in effect rejecting her without actually saying the words. Mariah set aside the carafe and took a sip of brandy before she crossed the room to where he stood. Lifting the snifter to his lips, she tipped it so that he could take a drink.

"Would you bring it into the bathroom?" he asked, his gaze openly curious as his eyes swept over her carefully arranged facial features.

"Of course." Mariah led the way, determined to handle the strain between them with dignity and calm. "You'll feel better once you're out of those clothes and clean again."

"I'll feel better when you start acting like yourself again," he remarked.

"I am," she insisted as she placed the snifter on the counter beside the sink.

"No, you're not."

He brushed aside her hands as she reached for the buttons on his denim shirt. "I can manage."

"No, you cannot manage," she snapped, too exasperated with him to be patient any longer. "You heard the paramedic. You aren't supposed to use your hands, so cooperate before I really lose my temper."

"I've never liked being dependent on anyone, Mariah. I'm not very good at it."

"I know that little fact better than anyone, Jack, especially after the last few weeks."

He studied her for a moment, then observed in a mild tone of voice, "You're very angry."

"Does that surprise you? Well, it shouldn't." She undid the shirt buttons while trying to hold on to her patience. Change the subject, she instructed herself. "I assume you tried to put out the fire yourself after you called for help."

He nodded as she peeled his shirt away from his body.

"Did you hear anything or anyone before you noticed the smoke?"

He shook his head. "I had the sander running."

Mariah pointed at the bench against the wall. Jack sat down without a word. She knelt in front of him and removed his shoes and socks. As she got to her feet he hooked his arm around her waist and stopped her from moving away from him.

"What are you doing, Mariah?"

Fighting the urge to wrap her arms around him and hold him, because she was so thankful that he hadn't been hurt in the fire, she hesitated for a moment before answering. "I'm helping you."

He stood suddenly, towering over her. "Why? You're furious with me."

Startled, she stared at him. "What does one have to do with the other?"

"Most people wouldn't be able to separate the two."

"I'm not most people."

"I'm finally starting to understand that."

Unnerved by his admission, Mariah concentrated on his belt buckle. Jack stepped back, evading her hands.

"I can take it from here," he said, "if you'll turn on the shower for me."

She stared at the dense hair that covered his chest, her fingers suddenly itching to slide through it. She wanted to feel his strength. She wanted the flex and flow of rippling muscles beneath her fingertips. She wanted him buried deep inside her, giving and receiving, sharing and loving. She wanted him to admit that he cared for her, even if the admission made him feel vulnerable. Didn't he think she felt vulnerable and uncertain? she wondered.

"I can take care of myself."

"Shut up, Jack," she said in a gentle voice. "You've been impossible lately. I've tried to be patient because I love you, but I'm tired of paying for something that someone must have done to you a long time ago."

He smiled. "It appears that I'm at your mercy now."

"Yes, you are. Is that so awful?"

He didn't answer her, but he surprised her by cooperating when she helped him disrobe. After turning on the water, she shed her clothes and followed him into the shower. She felt his gaze on her as she scrubbed the grime from his body and then washed his hair. She tried to ignore his arousal, but she failed. Each time she brushed against him, her inside melted a little more. Sensation skittered along her nerve endings, and an ache throbbed deep within her, expanding until it encompassed her entire body. She wanted him, but he seemed indifferent to his body's response.

When Mariah felt the shudder that suddenly rumbled through him, she realized that he wasn't impervious to her nakedness or her touch. He wanted her too. She felt certain of it, so she risked his rejection one more time as she drew his manhood into her hands and stroked him. His flesh swelled even more. She finally met his gaze, finally saw the glitter of desire in his dark eyes. He jerked free of her.

"I won't beg, Jack," she warned.

"Come here, Mariah."

He opened his arms to her. Following a moment of hesitation, she slipped between his powerful thighs, trapping his sex between their lower abdomens as she put her arms around his waist and arched upward into his strength and heat. He circled her shoulders with his arms.

"I apologize."

She looked up at him, still not feeling very calm, and taken aback by his remark. "It's about time. I think I deserve an explanation."

Jack tightened his embrace. "You're asking for something that's been impossible until now."

"I'm asking you to tell me why you don't trust me. I'm asking for the truth about your past, and this is the last time I intend to ask."

He chuckled. "You need children. You have all the right instincts for motherhood."

"Will you give me babies, Jack?"

Something primitive flared in his gaze. "We'll deal with that after we resolve a few other things. One thing at a time for now, all right? We still need to talk."

"You'll talk, and I'll listen, but first there's something I need to do."

"What's that, Vassar?"

"You, Jack. I need to do you," she whispered as she drew his head down, fastened her lips to his, and showed him the depth of her desire for him.

Mariah felt bold. She felt desired. And she felt more aware of her femininity than ever before. As she worked her way down the front of Jack's body, she used her fingertips, her open palms, and her mouth to convey her desire. She didn't stop until Jack trembled with the need for release.

She gave him that gift, trusting her instincts and expressing her love as she pushed him past the edge of his usual control. He shuddered violently, his body responding to her seduction and her loving.

He finally sagged back against the wall, his arms around Mariah once she stood. She leaned against him, content for the moment. They stood there until he regained his strength. Mariah sensed that they'd reached a turning point, but she cautioned herself against having any false hope.

After they rinsed off, Mariah slipped into a heavy terry robe and helped Jack towel dry. A few minutes later she sat beside him once he stretched out atop her bed. They shared what remained of the brandy in the snifter. Mariah waited for him to start talking. He finally did.

"You were right when you said you'd been paying for someone else's actions. I've been bitter and angry for years over what happened with Delia."

"Has that finally changed?" she asked.

"It has to change, or I'll lose you for good. I don't want that to happen, Mariah."

"So this whole situation involves your ex-wife and the reasons why your marriage ended?"

He looked pensive, then nodded. "It involves Darren too."

"I don't understand the connection."

"They were lovers."

Shocked, Mariah stared at him. The idea that his wife and his brother had betrayed him repulsed her. It was the kind of thing, she sensed, that Jack wouldn't ever be able to forgive. "I honestly don't know what to say, except that I'm sorry that you went through so much pain."

"There's more. Once I pieced together the puzzle, I realized that their affair had gone on during the first year of your marriage to Darren.

I found out . . ." He exhaled, his eyes closing for a moment. "I found out about their relationship during the divorce, but that was only part of what killed our marriage. Delia always insisted that she wanted children, but she seemed to have trouble getting pregnant. She lied and said she'd been tested. I went into my doctor for tests, and he assured me that I was fine. I didn't pressure her, because I knew we had plenty of time. She did get pregnant, though, but she had an abortion. It was Darren's child, I later learned, not mine. I found out quite accidentally, but after speaking to the doctor who performed the surgery and after confronting Delia, I discovered that she'd never had any intention of having children with me. I couldn't forgive her for the lies, the abortion, or for the fact that she'd had at least one affair, probably more. She refused to reveal the identity of her lover at first, but the truth came out at my lawyer's office. She wasn't happy with the settlement I'd offered her, and she lost her temper. I guess she decided that I hadn't been through enough, so she delivered her parting blow by announcing that my stepbrother was her lover. Darren was the lover who'd gotten her pregnant."

"He had several affairs during our marriage," she told him quietly. "He talked about the women when he drank too much, but he never used their names. He took great pleasure in telling me that I was as responsive as a rock in bed, so he needed other women."

Mariah saw the strain on his face, but she knew from personal experience that he needed to talk it through once and for all, no matter how excruciating the process. Speaking about Darren no longer roused bitter feelings in her, but her heart broke for Jack, because he hadn't had any help through the most painful episode in his life. "I always knew he lacked a conscience, but I would have expected him to feel some sense of loyalty to you."

"Neither one of them did. They weren't capable of those kinds of feelings, nor were they ever sensitive to the needs of others. They're both missing several essential elements that make a person whole. Elements like honor, integrity, and respect."

"You rejected me, because you didn't want to risk being betrayed again. Is that what's been going on?"

"I do love you, Mariah."

"But you keep pushing me away."

"I have a hard time with trust. Loving someone is like giving that person a powerful weapon to use against me."

"Do you think that's what I'd do?"

"Not any longer."

"What's changed?" she asked gently. His answer was very important.

"Me," he answered honestly. "I can't go on the way I have been. I won't lose you, Mariah. I need you in my life. I love you more than I thought I could ever love anyone."

She slipped down beside him on the bed. Molding herself against his naked body, she propped her chin on his shoulder and looked at him. "I will never betray you. I may make you angry, I may be busier than you'd like me to be with the foundation, but I will never betray you."

"I know that now, Vassar. I don't have any doubts about you. The person I doubt is myself. I've been too hard on you."

She arched an eyebrow. "Didn't I stand up for myself?"

He smiled. "Like a champ."

"You've met your match, Jack McMillan."

"If your performance in the shower is any indication, I believe you."

She sobered. "I remember the way you looked at her when you were at my wedding."

"I was obsessed with her."

"You seemed to love her."

"I thought so at the time. Now I don't think so. I think real love is more substantial, because what I feel for you makes me believe that I'll be happy for the rest of my life if we're together. I never felt secure with Delia. Being with her was like running in a race I couldn't win. I never seemed able to do enough to make her happy."

He pressed a kiss to Mariah's forehead, then levered himself up onto his elbow. She shifted onto her back and smiled up at him.

"What are you thinking now?" she asked.

"I'm thinking that you rescued me, so you're stuck with me."

"Is that so?" she breathed, her blue eyes bright with delight. "Does that mean you'll be at my mercy for a long time?"

His smiled faded. "Marry me and find out for yourself."

Mariah stared. "Marry you?"

He nodded. "Marry me, make a home with me here in Santa Barbara. We'll work it out so that you won't have a problem running the foundation."

"Why should we marry?"

"I think our children would appreciate it," he answered in a wry tone of voice. "I love you, Mariah. I always will."

"Forever and for always," she whispered, remembering a line from a love poem she'd once read.

"Forever, Vassar, and for always," Jack vowed as he leaned down and claimed her mouth.

When their lips finally parted, she responded to his proposal. "I'll marry you in the gazebo of the mansion when all the roses are in bloom." Jack smiled, clearly satisfied with her reply.

THE EDITOR'S CORNER

Along with the May flowers come six fabulous Love-swepts that will dazzle you with humor, excitement, and, above all, love. Touching, tender, packed with emotion and wonderfully happy endings, our six upcoming romances are real treasures.

The ever-popular Charlotte Hughes leads things off with **THE DEVIL AND MISS GOODY TWO-SHOES**, LOVESWEPT #684. Kane Stoddard had never answered the dozens of letters Melanie Abercrombie had written him in prison, but her words had kept his spirit alive during the three years he'd been jailed in error—and now he wants nothing more than a new start, and a chance to meet the woman who touched his angry soul. Stunned by the sizzling attraction she feels for Kane, Mel struggles to deny the passionate emotions Kane's touch awakens. No one had ever believed in Kane until Mel's sweet caring makes him dare to taste her innocent lips, makes him hunger to hold her until the sun rises. He can only hope that his fierce loving will vanquish her fear of losing him. Touching and intense, **THE DEVIL AND MISS GOODY TWO-SHOES** is the kind of love story that Charlotte is known and loved for.

This month Terry Lawrence delivers some **CLOSE ENCOUNTERS**, LOVESWEPT #685—but of the romantic kind. Alone in the elevator with his soon-to-be ex-wife, Tony Paretti decides he isn't giving Sara Cohen up without a fight! But when fate sends the elevator plunging ten floors and tosses her into his arms, he seizes his chance—and with breath-stealing abandon embraces the woman he's never stopped loving. Kissing Sara with a savage passion that transcends pain, Tony insists that what they had was too good to let go, that together they are strong enough to face the grief that shattered their marriage. Sara aches to rebuild the bonds of their love but doesn't know if she can trust him with her sorrow, even after Tony confesses the secret hopes that he's never dared to tell another soul. Terry will have you crying and cheering as these two people discover the courage to love again.

Get ready for a case of mistaken identity in **THE ONE FOR ME**, LOVESWEPT #686, by Mary Kay McComas. It was a ridiculous masquerade, pretending to be his twin brother at a business dinner, but Peter Wesley grows utterly confused when his guest returns from the powder room—and promptly steals his heart! She looks astonishingly like the woman he'd dined with earlier, but he's convinced that the cool fire and passionate longing in her bright blue eyes is new and dangerously irresistible. Katherine Asher hates impersonating her look-alike sisters, and seeing Peter makes her regret she'd ever agreed. When he kisses her with primitive yearning, she aches to admit her secret—that she wants him for herself! Once the charade is revealed, Peter woos her with fierce pleasure until she surrenders. She has always taken her happiness last, but is she ready to put her love for him first? **THE ONE FOR ME** is humorous and hot—just too good to resist.

Marcia Evanick gives us a hero who is **PLAYING FOR KEEPS**, LOVESWEPT #687. For the past two years detective Reece Carpenter has solved the fake murder-mystery at the Montgomery clan's annual family reunion, infuriating the beautiful—and competitive—Tennessee Montgomery. But when he faces his tempting rival this time, all he wants to win is her heart! Tennie has come prepared to beat her nemesis if it kills her—but the wild flames in his eyes light a fire in her blood that only his lips can satisfy. Tricked into working as a team, Tennie and Reece struggle to prove which is the better sleuth, but the enforced closeness creates a bigger challenge: to keep their minds on the case when they can't keep their hands off each other! Another keeper from Marcia Evanick.

STRANGE BEDFELLOWS, LOVESWEPT #688, is the newest wonderful romance from Patt Bucheister. John Lomax gave up rescuing ladies in distress when he traded his cop's mean streets for the peace of rural Kentucky, but he feels his resolve weaken when he discovers Silver Knight asleep on his couch! Her sea nymph's eyes brimming with delicious humor, her temptress's smile teasingly seductive, Silver pleads with him to probe a mystery in her New York apartment—and her hunk of a hero is hooked! Fascinated by her reluctant knight, an enigmatic warrior whose pain only she can soothe, Silver wonders if a joyous romp might help her free his spirit from the demons of a shadowy past. He is her reckless gamble, the dare she can't refuse—but she needs to make him understand his true home is in her arms. **STRANGE BEDFELLOWS** is Patt Bucheister at her sizzling best.

And last, but certainly not least, is **NO PROMISES MADE**, LOVESWEPT #689, by Maris Soule. Eric Newman is a sleek black panther of a man who holds Ashley Kehler spellbound, mesmerizing her with a look that strips her bare and caresses her senses, but he could also make her lose control, forget the dreams that drive her . . . and Ashley knows she must resist this seducer who ignites a fever in her blood! Drawn to this golden spitfire who is his opposite in every way, Eric feels exhilarated, intrigued against his will—but devastated by the knowledge that she'll soon be leaving. Ashley wavers between ecstasy and guilt, yet Eric knows the only way to keep his love is to let her go, hoping that she is ready to choose the life that will bring her joy. Don't miss this fabulous story!

Happy reading!

With warmest wishes,

Nita Taublib

Nita Taublib

Associate Publisher

P.S. Don't miss the exciting women's novels from Bantam that are coming your way in May—**DECEPTION**, by Amanda Quick, is the paperback edition of her first *New York Times* bestselling hardcover; **RELENTLESS**, by award-winning author Patricia Potter, is a searing tale of revenge and desire, set in Colorado during the 1870's; **SEIZED BY LOVE**, by Susan Johnson, is a novel of savage passions and dangerous pleasures sweeping from fabulous country estates and hunting lodges to the opulent ballrooms and salons of Russian nobility; and **WILD CHILD**, by bestselling author Suzanne Forster, reunites adversaries who share a tangled past—and for whom an old spark of conflict will kindle into a dangerously passionate blaze. We'll be giving you a sneak peek at these terrific books in next month's LOVESWEPTs. And immediately following this page look for a preview of the exciting romances from Bantam that are *available now*!

Don't miss these exciting books by your
favorite Bantam authors

On sale in March:

DARK PARADISE
by Tami Hoag

WARRIOR BRIDE
by Tamara Leigh

REBEL IN SILK
by Sandra Chastain

"Ms. Hoag has deservedly become one of the romance genre's most treasured authors."
—*Rave Reviews*

Look For

DARK PARADISE
by
Tami Hoag

Here is nationally bestselling author Tami Hoag's most dangerously erotic novel yet, a story filled with heart-stopping suspense and shocking passion . . . a story of a woman drawn to a man as hard and untamable as the land he loves, and to a town steeped in secrets—where a killer lurks.

Night had fallen by the time Mari finally found her way to Lucy's place with the aid of the map Lucy had sent in her first letter. Her "hide-out," she'd called it. The huge sky was as black as velvet, sewn with the sequins of more stars than she had ever imagined. The world suddenly seemed a vast, empty wilderness, and she pulled into the yard of the small ranch, questioning for the first time the wisdom of a surprise arrival. There were no lights glowing a welcome in the windows of the handsome new log house. The garage doors were closed.

   She climbed out of her Honda and stretched, feeling exhausted and rumpled. The past two weeks had sapped her strength, the decisions she had made taking chunks of it at a time. The drive up from Sacramento had been accomplished in a twenty-four hour marathon with breaks for nothing more than the bathroom and truck stop burritos, and now the physical strain of that weighed her down like an anchor.

It had seemed essential that she get here as quickly as possible, as if she had been afraid her nerve would give out and she would succumb to the endless dissatisfaction of her life in California if she didn't escape immediately. The wild pendulum her emotions had been riding had left her feeling drained and dizzy. She had counted on falling into Lucy's care the instant she got out of her car, but Lucy didn't appear to be home, and disappointment sent the pendulum swinging downward again.

Foolish, really, she told herself, blinking back the threat of tears as she headed for the front porch. She couldn't have expected Lucy to know she was coming. She hadn't been able to bring herself to call ahead. A call would have meant an explanation of everything that had gone on in the past two weeks, and that was better made in person.

A calico cat watched her approach from the porch rail, but jumped down and ran away as she climbed the steps, its claws scratching the wood floor as it darted around the corner of the porch and disappeared. The wind swept down off the mountain and howled around the weathered outbuildings, bringing with it a sense of isolation and a vague feeling of desertion that Mari tried to shrug off as she raised a hand and knocked on the door.

No lights brightened the windows. No voice called out for her to keep her pants on.

She swallowed at the combination of disappointment and uneasiness that crowded at the back of her throat. Against her will, her eyes did a quick scan of the moon-shadowed ranch yard and the hills beyond. The place was in the middle of nowhere. She had driven through the small town of New Eden and gone miles into the wilderness, seeing no more than two other houses on the way—and those from a great distance.

She knocked again, but didn't wait for an answer before trying the door. Lucy had mentioned wildlife in her few letters. The four-legged, flea-scratching kind.

"Bears. I remember something about bears," she muttered, the nerves at the base of her neck wriggling at the possibility that there were a dozen watching her from the cover of darkness, sizing her up with their beady little eyes while their stomachs growled. "If it's all the same to you, Luce, I'd rather not meet one up close and personal while you're off doing the boot scootin' boogie with some cowboy."

Stepping inside, she fumbled along the wall for a light switch, then blinked against the glare of a dozen small bulbs artfully arranged in a chandelier of antlers. Her first thought was that Lucy's abysmal housekeeping talents had deteriorated to a shocking new low. The place was a disaster area, strewn with books, newspapers, note paper, clothing.

She drifted away from the door and into the great room that encompassed most of the first floor of the house, her brain stumbling to make sense of the contradictory information it was getting. The house was barely a year old, a blend of Western tradition and contemporary architectural touches. Lucy had hired a decorator to capture those intertwined feelings in the interior. But the western watercolor prints on the walls hung at drunken angles. The cushions had been torn from the heavy, overstuffed chairs. The seat of the red leather sofa had been slit from end to end. Stuffing rose up from the wound in ragged tufts. Broken lamps and shattered pottery littered the expensive Berber rug. An overgrown pothos had been ripped from its planter and shredded, and was strung across the carpet like strips of tattered green ribbon.

Not even Lucy was this big a slob.

Mari's pulse picked up the rhythm of fear. "Lucy?" she called, the tremor in her voice a vocal extension of the goosebumps that were pebbling her arms. The only answer was an ominous silence that pressed in on her eardrums until they were pounding.

She stepped over a gutted throw pillow, picked her way around a smashed terra cotta urn and peered into the darkened kitchen area. The refrigerator door was ajar, the light within glowing like the promise of gold inside a treasure chest. The smell, however, promised something less pleasant.

She wrinkled her nose and blinked against the sour fumes as she found the light switch on the wall and flicked it upward. Recessed lighting beamed down on a repulsive mess of spoiling food and spilled beer. Milk puddled on the Mexican tile in front of the refrigerator. The carton lay abandoned on its side. Flies hovered over the garbage like tiny vultures.

"Jesus, Lucy," she muttered, "what kind of party did you throw here?"

And where the hell are you?

The pine cupboard doors stood open, their contents spewed out of them. Stoneware and china and flatware lay broken and scattered. Appropriately macabre place settings for the gruesome meal that had been laid out on the floor.

Mari backed away slowly, her hand trembling as she reached out to steady herself with the one ladder-back chair that remained upright at the long pine harvest table. She caught her full lower lip between her teeth and stared through the sheen of tears. She had worked too many criminal cases not to see this for what it was. The house had been ransacked. The motive could have been robbery or the destruction could have been the aftermath of something else, something uglier.

"Lucy?" she called again, her heart sinking like a stone at the sure knowledge that she wouldn't get an answer.

Her gaze drifted to the stairway that led up to the loft where the bedrooms were tucked, then cut to the telephone that had been ripped from the kitchen wall and now hung by slender tendons of wire.

Her heart beat faster. A fine mist of sweat slicked her palms.

"Lucy?"

"She's dead."

The words were like a pair of shotgun blasts in the still of the room. Mari wheeled around, a scream wedged in her throat right behind her heart. He stood at the other end of the table, six feet of hewn granite in faded jeans and a chambray work shirt. How anything that big could have sneaked up on her was beyond reasoning. Her perceptions distorted by fear, she thought his shoulders rivaled the mountains for size. He stood there, staring at her from beneath the low-riding brim of a dusty black Stetson, his gaze narrow, measuring, his mouth set in a grim, compressed line. His right hand—big with blunt-tipped fingers—hung at his side just inches from a holstered revolver that looked big enough to bring down a buffalo.

WARRIOR BRIDE
by
Tamara Leigh

"... *a vibrant, passionate love story that captures all the splendor of the medieval era ... A sheer delight.*"
—*bestselling author Teresa Medeiros*

After four years of planning revenge on the highway-man who'd stolen her future, Lizanne Balmaine had the blackguard at the point of her sword. Yet some-thing about the onyx-eyed man she'd abducted and taken to her family estate was different—something that made her hesitate at her moment of triumph. Now she was his prisoner ... and even more than her handsome captor she feared her own treacherous desires.

"Welcome, my Lord Ranulf," she said. "'Tis a fine day for a duel."

He stared unblinkingly at her, then let a frown settle between his eyes. "Forsooth, I did not expect you to attend this bloodletting," he said. "I must needs remember you are not a lady."

Her jaw hardened. "I assure you I would not miss this for anything," she tossed back.

He looked at the weapons she carried. "And where is this man who would champion your ill-fated cause?" he asked, looking past her.

"Man?" She shook her head. "There is no man."

Ranulf considered this, one eyebrow arched. "You were unable to find a single man willing to die for you, my lady? Not one?"

Refusing to rise to the bait, Lizanne leaned forward, smiling faintly. "Alas, I fear I am so uncomely that none would offer."

"And what of our bargain?" Ranulf asked, suspicion cast upon his voice.

"It stands."

"You think to hold me till your brother returns?" He shifted more of his weight onto his uninjured leg. "Do you forget that I am an unwilling captive, my lady? 'Tis not likely you will return me to that foul-smelling cell." He took a step toward her.

At his sudden movement, the mare shied away, snorting loudly as it pranced sideways. Lizanne brought the animal under control with an imperceptible tightening of her legs.

"Nay," she said, her eyes never wavering. "Your opponent is here before you now."

Ranulf took some moments to digest this, then burst out laughing. As preposterous as it was, a mere woman challenging an accomplished knight to a duel of swords, her proposal truly did not surprise him, though it certainly amused him.

And she was not jesting! he acknowledged. Amazingly, it fit the conclusions he had wrestled with, and finally accepted, regarding her character.

Had she a death wish, then? Even if that spineless brother of hers had shown her how to swing a sword, it was inconceivable she could have any proficiency with such a heavy, awkward weapon. A sling, perhaps, and he mustn't forget a dagger, but a sword?

Slowly, he sobered, blinking back tears of mirth and drawing deep, ragged breaths of air.

She edged her horse nearer, her indignation evident in her stiffly erect bearing. "I find no humor in the situation. Mayhap you would care to enlighten me, Lord Ranulf?"

"Doubtless, you would not appreciate my explanation, my lady."

Her chin went up. "Think you I will not make a worthy opponent?"

"With your nasty tongue, perhaps, but—"

"Then let us not prolong the suspense any longer," she snapped. Swiftly, she removed the sword from its scabbard and tossed it, hilt first, to him.

Reflexively, Ranulf pulled it from the air, his hand closing around the cool metal hilt. He was taken aback as he held it aloft, for inasmuch as the weapon appeared perfectly honed on both its edges, it was not the weighty sword he was accustomed to. Indeed, it felt awkward in his grasp.

"And what is this, a child's toy?" he quipped, twisting the sword in his hand.

In one fluid motion, Lizanne dismounted and turned to face him. "'Tis the instrument of your death, my lord." Advancing, she drew her own sword, identical to the one he held.

He lowered his sword's point and narrowed his eyes. "Think you I would fight a woman?"

"'Tis as we agreed."

"I agreed to fight a man—"

"Nay, you agreed to fight the opponent of my choice. I stand before you now ready to fulfill our bargain."

"We have no such bargain," he insisted.

"Would you break your vow? Are you so dishonorable?"

Never before had Ranulf's honor been questioned. For King Henry and, when necessary, himself, he had fought hard and well, and he carried numerous battle scars to attest to his valor. Still, her insult rankled him.

"'Tis honor that compels me to decline," he

said, a decidedly dangerous smile playing about his lips.

"Honor?" She laughed, coming to an abrupt halt a few feet from him. "Methinks 'tis your injury, coward. Surely, you can still wield a sword?"

Coward? A muscle in his jaw jerked. This one was expert at stirring the remote depths of his anger. "Were you a man, you would be dead now."

"Then imagine me a man," she retorted, lifting her sword in challenge.

The very notion was laughable. Even garbed as she was, the Lady Lizanne was wholly a woman.

"Nay, I fear I must decline." Resolutely, he leaned on the sword. "'Twill make a fine walking stick, though," he added, flexing the steel blade beneath his weight.

Ignoring his quip, Lizanne took a step nearer. "You cannot decline!"

"Aye, and I do."

"Then I will gut you like a pig!" she shouted and leaped forward.

REBEL IN SILK
by
Sandra Chastain

*Dallas Burke had come to Willow Creek, Wyoming,
to find her brother's killer, and she had no intention of being scared off—not by the roughnecks who
trashed her newspaper office, nor by the devilishly
handsome cowboy who warned her of the violence to
come. Yet she couldn't deny that the tall, sunbronzed
rancher had given her something to think about,
namely, what it would be like to be held in his
steel-muscled arms and feel his sensuous mouth on
hers . . . .*

A bunch of liquored-up cowboys were riding past
the station, shooting guns into the air, bearing down
on the startled Miss Banning caught by drifts in the
middle of the street.

From the general store, opposite where Dallas
was standing, came a figure who grabbed her valise
in one hand and scooped her up with the other, flung her over his shoulder, and stepped onto
the wooden sidewalk beneath the roof over the
entrance to the saloon.

Dallas let out a shocked cry as the horses
thundered by. She might have been run over had
it not been for the man's quick action. Now,
hanging upside down, she felt her rescuer's hand

cradling her thigh in much too familiar a manner.

"Sir, what are you doing?"

"Saving your life."

The man lifted her higher, then, as she started to slide, gave her bottom another tight squeeze. Being rescued was one thing, but this was out of line. Gratitude flew out of her mind as he groped her backside.

"Put me down, you . . . you . . . lecher!"

"Gladly!" He leaned forward, loosened his grip and let her slide to the sidewalk where she landed in a puddle of melted snow and ice. The valise followed with a thump.

"Well, you didn't have to try to break my leg!" Dallas scrambled to her feet, her embarrassment tempering her fear and turning it into anger.

"No, I could have let the horses do it!"

Dallas had never heard such cold dispassion in a voice. He wasn't flirting with her. He wasn't concerned about her injuries. She didn't know why he'd bothered to touch her so intimately. One minute he was there, and the next he had turned to walk away.

"Wait, please wait! I'm sorry to appear ungrateful. I was just startled."

As she scurried along behind him, all she could see was the hat covering his face and head, his heavy canvas duster, and boots with silver spurs set with turquoise. He wasn't stopping.

Dallas reached out and caught his arm. "Now, just a minute. Where I come from, a man at least gives a lady the chance to say a proper thank you. What kind of man are you?"

"I'm cold, I'm thirsty, and I'm ready for a woman. Are you volunteering?"

There was a snickering sound that ran through the room they'd entered. Dallas raised her head and glanced around. She wasn't the only woman in the saloon, but she was the only one wearing all her clothes.

Any other woman might have gasped. But Dallas suppressed her surprise. She didn't know the layout of the town yet, and until she did, she wouldn't take a chance of offending anyone, even these ladies of pleasure. "I'm afraid not. I'm a newspaperwoman, not a . . . an entertainer."

He ripped his hat away, shaking off the glistening beads of melting snow that hung in the jet-black hair that touched his shoulders. He was frowning at her, his brow drawn into deep lines of displeasure; his lips, barely visible beneath a bushy mustache, pressed into a thin line.

His eyes, dark and deep, held her. She sensed danger and a hot intensity.

Where the man she'd met on the train seemed polished and well-mannered, her present adversary was anything but a gentleman. He was a man of steel who challenged with every glance. She shivered in response.

"Hello," a woman's voice intruded. "I'm Miranda. You must have come in on the train."

Dallas blinked, breaking the contact between her and her rescuer. With an effort, she turned to the woman.

"Ah, yes. I did. Dallas Banning." She started to hold out her hand, realized that she was clutching her valise, then lowered it. "I'm afraid I've made rather a mess of introducing myself to Green Willow Creek."

"Well, I don't know about what happened in the street, but following Jake in here might give your reputation a bit of a tarnish."

"Jake?" This was the Jake that her brother Jamie had been worried about.

"Why, yes," Miranda said, "I assumed you two knew each other?"

"Not likely," Jake growled and turned to the bar. "She's too skinny and her mouth is too big for my taste."

"Miss Banning?" Elliott Parnell, the gentleman she'd met on the train, rushed in from the street. "I saw what happened. Are you all right?"

Jake looked up, catching Dallas between him and the furious look he cast at Elliott Parnell.

Dallas didn't respond. The moment Jake had spotted Mr. Elliott, everything in the saloon had seemed to stop. All movement. All sound. For a long endless moment it seemed as if everyone in the room were frozen in place.

Jake finally spoke. "If she's with you and your sodbusters, Elliott, you'd better get her out of here."

Elliot took Dallas's arm protectively. "No, Jake. We simply came in on the same train. Miss Banning is James Banning's sister."

"Oh? The troublemaking newspaper editor. Almost as bad as the German immigrants. I've got no use for either one. Take my advice, Miss Banning. Get on the next train back to wherever you came from."

"I don't need your advice, Mr. Silver."

"Suit yourself, but somebody didn't want your brother here, and my guess is that you won't be any more welcome!"

Dallas felt a shiver of pure anger ripple down her backbone. She might as well make her position known right now. She came to find out the truth and she wouldn't be threatened. "Mr. Silver—"

"Jake! Elliott!" Miranda interrupted, a warning in her voice. "Can't you see that Miss Banning is half-frozen? Men! You have to forgive them," she said, turning to Dallas. "At the risk of further staining your reputation, I'd be pleased to have you make use of my room to freshen up and get dry. That is if you don't mind being . . . here."

"I'd be most appreciative, Miss Miranda," Dallas said, following her golden-haired hostess to the stairs.

Dallas felt all the eyes in the room boring holes in her back. She didn't have to be told where she was and what was taking place beyond the doors on either side of the corridor. If being here ruined her reputation, so be it. She wasn't here to make friends anyway. Besides, a lead to Jamie's murderer was a lot more likely to come from these people than those who might be shocked by her actions.

For just a second she wondered what would have happened if Jake had marched straight up the stairs with her. Then she shook off the impossible picture that thought had created.

She wasn't here to be bedded.

She was here to kill a man.

She just had to find out which one.

OFFICIAL RULES

To enter the sweepstakes below carefully follow all instructions found elsewhere in this offer.

The **Winners Classic** will award prizes with the following approximate maximum values: 1 Grand Prize: $26,500 (or $25,000 cash alternate); 1 First Prize: $3,000; 5 Second Prizes: $400 each; 35 Third Prizes: $100 each; 1,000 Fourth Prizes: $7.50 each. Total maximum retail value of Winners Classic Sweepstakes is $42,500. Some presentations of this sweepstakes may contain individual entry numbers corresponding to one or more of the aforementioned prize levels. To determine the Winners, individual entry numbers will first be compared with the winning numbers preselected by computer. For winning numbers not returned, prizes will be awarded in random drawings from among all eligible entries received. Prize choices may be offered at various levels. If a winner chooses an automobile prize, all license and registration fees, taxes, destination charges and, other expenses not offered herein are the responsibility of the winner. If a winner chooses a trip, travel must be complete within one year from the time the prize is awarded. Minors must be accompanied by an adult. Travel companion(s) must also sign release of liability. Trips are subject to space and departure availability. Certain black-out dates may apply.

The following applies to the sweepstakes named above:

No purchase necessary. You can also enter the sweepstakes by sending your name and address to: P.O. Box 508, Gibbstown, N.J. 08027. Mail each entry separately. Sweepstakes begins 6/1/93. Entries must be received by 12/30/94. Not responsible for lost, late, damaged, misdirected, illegible or postage due mail. Mechanically reproduced entries are not eligible. All entries become property of the sponsor and will not be returned.

Prize Selection/Validations: Selection of winners will be conducted no later than 5:00 PM on January 28, 1995, by an independent judging organization whose decisions are final. Random drawings will be held at 1211 Avenue of the Americas, New York, N.Y. 10036. Entrants need not be present to win. Odds of winning are determined by total number of entries received. Circulation of this sweepstakes is estimated not to exceed 200 million. All prizes are guaranteed to be awarded and delivered to winners. Winners will be notified by mail and may be required to complete an affidavit of eligibility and release of liability which must be returned within 14 days of date on notification or alternate winners will be selected in a random drawing. Any prize notification letter or any prize returned to a participating sponsor, Bantam Doubleday Dell Publishing Group, Inc., its participating divisions or subsidiaries, or the independent judging organization as undeliverable will be awarded to an alternate winner. Prizes are not transferable. No substitution for prizes except as offered or as may be necessary due to unavailability, in which case a prize of equal or greater value will be awarded. Prizes will be awarded approximately 90 days after the drawing. All taxes are the sole responsibility of the winners. Entry constitutes permission (except where prohibited by law) to use winners' names, hometowns, and likenesses for publicity purposes without further or other compensation. Prizes won by minors will be awarded in the name of parent or legal guardian.

Participation: Sweepstakes open to residents of the United States and Canada, except for the province of Quebec. Sweepstakes sponsored by Bantam Doubleday Dell Publishing Group, Inc., (BDD), 1540 Broadway, New York, NY 10036. Versions of this sweepstakes with different graphics and prize choices will be offered in conjunction with various solicitations or promotions by different subsidiaries and divisions of BDD. Where applicable, winners will have their choice of any prize offered at level won. Employees of BDD, its divisions, subsidiaries, advertising agencies, independent judging organization, and their immediate family members are not eligible.

Canadian residents, in order to win, must first correctly answer a time limited arithmetical skill testing question. Void in Puerto Rico, Quebec and wherever prohibited or restricted by law. Subject to all federal, state, local and provincial laws and regulations. For a list of major prize winners (available after 1/29/95): send a self-addressed, stamped envelope entirely separate from your entry to: Sweepstakes Winners, P.O. Box 517, Gibbstown, NJ 08027. Requests must be received by 12/30/94. DO NOT SEND ANY OTHER CORRESPONDENCE TO THIS P.O. BOX.